A Talisman in the Darkness

A Talisman in the Darkness

Stories by Olga Orozco

Translated by Mary G. Berg and Melanie Nicholson

White Pine Press / Buffalo, New York

White Pine Press
P.O. Box 236
Buffalo, New York 14201

www.whitepine.org

Acknowledgments: "The Dwarves" appeared in an earlier version in *Puerto del Sol,* volume 37 (2002). "Mission Accomplished" appeared in an earlier version in *Translation Review,* volume 77-78 (2009).
Publication of this book was made possible, in part, by grants from the National Endowment of the Arts, which believes that a great nation deserves great art, and with public funds from the New York State Council on the Arts, a State Agency.

First Edition.

ISBN: 978-1-935210-30-6

Printed and bound in the United States of America.

Library of Congress Control Number: 2011931994

Contents

Introduction

By the time of her death in 1999, Olga Orozco was widely recognized as one of Latin America's most important twentieth-century poets. Her poetry, oracular in tone and surrealistic in vision, has received considerable critical attention and has been widely anthologized and translated into numerous languages. Yet Orozco's fiction, collected in two volumes of short stories whose settings and characters intertwine and enrich each other, has remained until now a fairly well-guarded secret. The present collection, comprised of stories from *La oscuridad es otro sol* (Darkness Is Another Sun, 1967) and *También la luz es un abismo* (Light Also Is an Abyss, 1993), introduces English-speaking readers to the hallucinatory yet lucid world that Orozco's young narrator, Lía, inhabits and animates with her prodigious imagination.

Orozco was born in 1920 in Toay, a small town on the Argentine pampa. She later moved to Bahía Blanca and eventually to Buenos Aires, where she made her career as a poet and journalist. But it is the landscape of her childhood home that shapes her narrative voice. In this mirage-like world of shifting dunes, shimmering horizons, crumbling buildings and vibrating fields of sunflowers, the young girl Lía—Orozco's alter ego—watches and wonders, acts and is acted upon. Fixed in the center of the erratic exterior world is the family home, the refuge to which the child retreats for protection and solace, but which at times resembles a space of mystery and menace.

From the grandmother who chastises God in her prayers, to the older brother Alejandro, whose death gives Lía the first image of her own mortality, to the older sister Laura, mischievous and courageous and loyal, the family that surrounds Lía assures her of her place in the world without ever simplifying its contours. At the borders of the family domain wander the stories' other characters, delicately balanced between the fantastical and the humanly vulnerable. There is the Best Spy Organization in the World and Its Surroundings, a band of children—including Lía and Laura—who roam the town during the afternoon siesta, uncovering sometimes frightening truths about their neighbors and about each other, about friendship and eroticism and death. There is Nanni, the failed Italian opera singer who has made his temporary home in the granary, singing his broken arias and reconstructing for the children a heroic version of his ignominious role as an extra. There is María Teo, the village seamstress, fortune teller, and secret practitioner of voodoo, whom Lía's Aunt Adelaide both despises and reveres. There are the colorful gypsies who set up camp in the vacant lot across the road, repairing pots and pans, selling wares, and—Lía fears—stealing children.

In each of these scenarios, the reality of small-town life on the Argentine plains in the 1920s is filtered through the consciousness of the narrator-protagonist Lía, the child whose stories are both hers and those of her Other, her grown-up self. The prose that results from this double voice is rich in imagery—Orozco remains a poet, even as she writes fiction—and is marked by wonder, fascination, superstition, bewilderment, anguish, nostalgia, recognition, and sometimes a reluctant wisdom. Though a rural form of Catholicism shapes Lía's understanding (Orozco's family was Basque, Irish, and Sicilian in origin), the writer's later incursions into esoteric belief systems, particularly Gnosticism, add an overlay of unconventional spirituality to the child's attempts to make sense of her world.

The prose style of Orozco's stories is extremely subjective and impressionistic, making the task of translation both exhilarating and challenging. The narrative complexity is twofold. First, Lía faces real occurrences—the discovery of a dead man's body by the railroad tracks, an unsettling visit to the town's fortune-teller, the exploration of a haunted house—that constantly challenge her sense of the world as a structured and predictable place. Second, her own imagination is capable of taking a simple impression or event and transforming it into a multifarious, confounding, and threatening assault on the self. In either case, the result is a stream-of-consciousness prose structure characterized by long sentences, multiple embedded clauses, metaphors built upon metaphors, and unexpected imagistic juxtapositions, all of which demand precision on the part of the translator and unflagging attention on the part of the reader.

One striking example of this impressionistic narrative approach occurs in the story "And Still the Wheel." In this story, Lía is being carried on horseback by Grandpa Damián home to Toay from the nearby town of Telén. The backdrop to this situation—her brother Alejandro's death and the family's decision to remove Lía from the immediate realities of this event—add to her confusion and fear. All that she sees and experiences on this wild gallop home is altered by her heightened emotional state:

> The horse neighs, rears up, shakes its head nervously, refuses to go on. Something is coming close. Something comes rolling down the road without any wheel. Between two eye-blinks of lightning I can just make out a shadowy shape. It's a huge, brownish, spiny figure, made of air and aggression. It comes closer, slight and unsteady, lacking skin or heart, and thus apparently lacking mystery. But it belongs to the world of unfathomable, outward repetition, to the world of unintentional and blind threat—maybe the most dangerous kind, since the most forceful denial operates everywhere, but invisibly. I wonder from what distance it orders this messenger of fate to reach out of the void, to envelop and incorporate us like water, shadow, or stain. Let it come then, let it invade us, let it change us into another appendage identical to the rest of its stiff nothingness. Horse, old man, and child: we'll keep moving inside another wheel of uncontrolled and irreversible fate, whose center will continue to spin simply with the hands of the clock, until the absurd universe is absurdly consummated. But no. It brushes past us and goes on its way. And so it will grow in its aridity, gathering other identical shapes into its outsized bulk, other shapes equally uprooted and directionless. I have known atrocious moments that look exactly like this thing. (31)

The paragraph ends and the reader still does not know what "this thing" could be. But in Orozco's fiction, this sort of complex verbal and imagistic construction typically resolves itself into a graspable psychic event, signaling at least a momentary understanding on Lía's part: "Grandpa Damián says simply: 'That was a tumbleweed.'" Orozco skillfully crafts the passage to allow the reader to experience the "Aha!" moment exactly as Lía does. The narrative rhythm shifts at such junctures: the prose relaxes, events are narrated sequentially, descriptions are straightforward...until the next specter arises before Lía's eyes. These shadowy projections and the subsequent moments of lucidity that mark the narrator's brief epiphanies make reading Orozco's stories an unpredictable but powerful experience.

The tumbleweed is one of a series of mysterious and very possibly menacing circular spots, wheels, or blotches, interrelated in the child's perceptions by the familiar (but scary) children's game of tag, called in Argentina *la mancha venenosa,* the poisonous blotch, where the person who is It tries to pass on the "poisonous affliction" by tagging someone else, who then becomes the carrier of this ominous black plague. Lía's recurrent fear is associated with the death of her brother Alejandro. She is haunted by the image of his "face, the one that kept spinning in the wheels of the carriage with its color of no return." (27) Recurrently she imagines herself within a terrifying "wheel of fire" or menaced by fragments of memory, spinning bits of undigested recollections, "more and more distorted ... in that shining, dizzy, bedeviled circle" (128) often a red-tinged ominous horror signifying "tremulous and oppressive danger."(66)

Orozco's stories recreate a South American childhood that readers will find startling, haunting, and visually resplendent. But they do more. They offer a sober and lyrical reflection on the writer's struggle to see, to step beyond contingency and into the absolute. The final story of her second (and last) collection of stories, "The Goodbyes," recalls the family's move away from the town of Toay. Here the simulated child's vision is brought into perfect equilibrium with the world view of the older writer. The terror and allure of the unknown, which have never left her, are projected from the road leading out of Toay onto the trajectory of an entire lifetime:

> Here everything is done to bear the light through the shadow that spreads, and its full presence is only manifest in a flash of lightning, because it is not on this side. I am terrified by the single thought of trying to seize the illumination or full knowledge by hurling myself in one leap into an illusory bottomless clarity. It's like hoping to see the unknown face-on, from the center of a diamond, or like being a prisoner, incrusted in a blinding glacier, or worse yet, like leaping into

> an unbearable, hallucinatory brilliance, through which I fall and fall going nowhere, with no talisman, without a sacred thread, without a love stone clutched in my fist. Against the false light that makes it impossible to see, I choose the invisible. Is that because the light also is an abyss? (165–66)

Orozco's lifelong search for gnosis, for the sudden gleam that will reveal the "other side," is recognized here as yet another mirage or source of disillusionment. Yet the passage suggests that the worst fear is that of "falling and falling" within that light, without a sacred object to protect her. What might that object be? Orozco speaks in one of her poems of "my words, my only talisman in the darkness." These stories, then, alongside her abundant production of poetry, are Orozco's talisman, the gift of a stone clutched in a child's fist that she quietly passes to us.

A Talisman in the Darkness

Once Upon a Time

. . .

There was once a house—no. At one time there was a house—no. At certain times there were certain houses that were one house. Was it really a house, or was it a mirror forged by the three times, so that each time was the consequence of and the motive for the other? As in a kaleidoscope, maybe, or a many-sided self like a dressing room where the one who's going to be, wearing an old woman's mask, can try on the mask of the one who was, wearing the child's mask, and vice versa and so on and so on. The mask of the one who is and that can only be seen from within, from the backside of all the masks merged into one, until that object we usually call a face devours itself and we see who is devouring it, and then I suppose I'll prove my suspicion: that no one is a single self, but all the successive selves in one.

But right now time is, and apparently I am I, myself alone. In this moment when I'm going to be born, when I'm going to go back, both time and the person are *I am.* And the house is there, like a moonstone where steam is rarefied to the boiling point, then condenses into bubbles that suck me into the core of a buried ember where I will enter so eternity will not be interrupted, so I can continue this rocking with which I set forth from who-knows-where and throw myself face-first into the void against the panes of darkness.

I've arrived. Facing the threshold there is a sand dune that must pass through the eye of a needle, and behind it a garden where the roots of death begin. I still don't know how to speak. When I learn, I will have forgotten the road that brought me here.

The gate opens onto that interior that from now on will be the outside. There are faces in the windows waiting for me. There are figures who watch: one part solidified in the frost that still holds me; the other part burning in the lamps we'll hold when we go. Grandmother, Papa, Mama, Aunt Adelaida, and my brothers and sisters: Alejandro, María de las Nieves, Laura. Of the many that were, only two are left. Perhaps they'll be here until I go. Metal birds with their sharp voices call out Who? Who? Who? from high up in the eaves.

"It's me, Lía. Only Lía, coming back from the future."

From the dovecote that blocks my path the gold-breasted ringdove answers: "There's no one, no one, no one." I blow on it and it dissolves. Behind it is the door. I don't need a key to enter. I haven't lost my innocence. I've seen it written on the tablets of a different law. I push. A great wall appears, watching me with blind eyes.

"The map, the map made of dampness and ashen mildew where I'll decipher my destiny on many walls."

I can't stay here. I should look for the door. A step backwards and there's the void I tumble into each night, latching onto a scrap of faith that envelops me, like a sheet I wrap around me or like dragging along the naves of a cathedral that's become a collapsed sky.

"At the end of every path there is a garden," I repeat as I fall.

"Mama, Mother!" I shout, and she drags me toward the parlor reserved for visitors and wakes. "Why am I here?" "Because children are born." "How are they born?" "A man and a woman are joined together." "Forever?" "Yes, forever, because forever is an eternity, generation after generation." And she shows me an alphabet whose code is buried somewhere unknown to her or to my grandmother, or to my grandmother's mother, or her mother. No one will inherit it from me. I'll be the first to mistrust the trap of my condition. It will be dissolved in my blood: a red, b vermillion, c ruby, d garnet, e purple, f scarlet, and so on to the end.

"Papa, Father!" I shout. And he drags me toward the spiral staircase, toward the hallway of many doors that open and close again. "Why am I here?" "I don't know. No one expected you." "Then why?" "A man and a woman are joined together." "Forever?" "No, forever is a moment of never, generation after generation." And he shows me a calculation that means nothing beyond him, not even to my grandfather, nor my grandfather's father, nor his father before him. No one will inherit it from me. I'll be the first to enjoy the freedom of their condition. It will be resolved in my blood: 1+1=2, 2-1=1, 1+1=2, 2-1=1, and so on until the end.

And at the end of each hallway the door reappears, the one that opens to reveal a vein structure glowing from bottom to top along the leaf that trembles in the night storm while I also tremble, but inside there's a warmth I'll seek elsewhere in vain when I approach to rest my head beside the seven heads bent over a book of illustrations that's beginning to turn into an album of faded photographs or a crystal ball for peering into the future because the little blue-hooded girl has been left alone with her awe and her fear under the snowflakes that are swirling around the snowman that will last until spring, until the faded yellow of birth certificates that no one carried with them when they left in the car that in my memory blends into a coach covered with flowers for the Day of the Dead, which moves down the dizzy checkerboard pattern of the tiled carriageway and becomes fused with that other coach in which I leave for my encounter with the irredeemable unknown, moving toward the irredeemable solitude that's behind each face that I call out to with its final name so it will go away when it no longer feels the same tormented desperation of having to leave two minutes later with the same she-wolf's hunger with which I fight for the portion of unhappiness that falls to me instead of to habit, instead of pity for caressing my head in the mirror of the first communion, enemy of the miracle or the backwards miracle in which I trust while I'm facing that field of sunflowers I'll have to leave deep down in the cellar, even if I'm sometimes awakened bodily by my mother's hand that was left forever beneath the roots of a rosebush after having rocked me with a rocking that I still repeat in a goodbye while I leave on the train dressed up like a traveler on her way to happiness who slips through the trap door down to these four walls smelling of pine that open onto a sea spotted like a tiger trapped in a cage where once again I enumerate my invulnerable anatomy, the same one crossing so many ages covered with the same skin beneath other hands, one hand for winning and the other for losing, and it always comes out the same even if I've bet the future on a game called Ever Never among the little stones I keep as my only prize in the bureau drawer where the lamp of fireflies gathered under eucalyptus trees in the park burns endlessly in its velvet-lined box surrounded by a smell that tosses me into the crumpled sheets of a bed where in the midst of my fever I can see my father's face crying over the vanished face of my brother Alejandro who rides away in Elijah's chariot leaving me this face that I unintentionally stole, perhaps at the same moment when I myself returned from death four years before, having passed from a tub of freezing water for heaven to a tub of boiling mustard for hell, not a basin where I wet my feet so I can die after the first punishment reflected in the silver teapot where one is elongated in a flame that consumes itself surrounded by red wallpaper and the oak of a dining room that I've known since birth and in which I'm seated in the middle of the island to celebrate this new year in which no one tells me Lía take your twelve bitter green grapes, one for each month of the year for thirty two years so they can be picked the way Grandmother picks her rosary beads under the oxygen tent, making signs that no one understands since they're not meant for this place, for this side of the wall where there's still a circle around the leprous letters GKY that could mean God Keep You beneath the wainscoting that smells of dust and crepe and the carnival costume, so alike from one sequin to another, from one pair of eyes to another, when you look at yourself in order to truly find them and not just to stay there in order to stay, and you take the dust cloud of the drought years so you can hide them embarrassed under the bed with the irons and bronzes to which you cling, crying, because you're a dwarf from head to toe and because each paradise recovered in a certain way is a paradise lost again among proper names on notebooks, always grasping the wooden bars, clinging to the talisman of faith in order to hoist myself up to the edge of nightmares and get out of the attic where they keep all the heads lopped off of every age, next to the mannequin with measurements that don't match anyone except maybe those transparent beings who take advantage of the clock chiming one and come down to the gilded living room where moths have turned the armchairs into habitable mummies where I'm supposed to sit facing the wall until I drown in the water of the majolica bowls in order to expiate my fall, which is everyone's fall, which is God's fall in everyone unable to judge him because he's the same God in transit until he realigns the heavens after a dissatisfaction with his initial perfection, since otherwise there would be no reason to hold him within, nullifying evil, nor any reason for having come here or for having to repeat history down to the final judgment which is his own judgment or rather that of everyone reintegrated into a unity of times and people, of transitive intransitive verbs untransited by the anesthesia of memory lost in the sand where Laura buried her seven-stranded ring to remember that it's better to forget, and I my baptismal medal with Our Lady of Perpetual Succor, to know with certainty that since then she comes only when one arrives at the far edge of the separation of deep waters because we have to pass through layers of pride all the way to the total absence of the left hand flayed by the right hand for which it searches or from which it flees beneath the pillow as if it were another plank of salvation or shipwreck and maybe it's another within oneself like another hand can be and it's the extension of our own nameless hand that says mine, not even in that moment when one sets out for the other coast to reach the beloved from this corner of the room to which we return inexplicably wrapped in a double skin with proof of separation, even if we've created this monster that devours us in the light of a certain lamp with fringes of green and pink mustard seeds that extend like a column of ants out to the lantern of a worm-eaten boat that is extinguished when someone lights the opalescent lamp and the brightness of all three stretches like a cloud from blind revelation to blind ignorance reflected in the cups of chocolate served on every birthday in the dawn-blue porcelain with a rose on the bottom in the winter fog that sticks to the windows where María de las Nieves appears dressed like a ghost with her best howl the better to torture me with, unaware that now that she's gone I would give my eyes that didn't want to see her if only she'd come back with the same suit she traded for the one she wore thirty years later, no matter when she might come back to tell me children are made out of the vapor rising from two uncorked bottles only to dissolve in the same way, and if only we could talk about all these objects jumbled in dresser drawers that end in a precise divvying up of the heart, awaiting a voice to awaken them to say amen so they can rise up by the spring of their secret life or fall to pieces with the awful noise of a crustacean smashing against the floor, now free of the fear of suffocation beneath the cascading lace that my grandmother embroiders with her guardian angel patience, alert at the edge of every insomnia into which I'm about to fall for having picked a blue flower where I watch the growth of hermetic organisms that surely ambush me from the place of what I might be, of what I hope not to be, since suddenly I'm struck by the fear that I still live to step beyond the boundaries of what I am so I can commit my crime, and maybe that's what keeps me from passing judgment in place of a compassion which is passion shared above all when I watch these hands that are so strange to me even when they have the authority of a will that may not even be mine, stretched out blandly over the tattoos of a school desk that lives on in this mahogany table where they lie palm-up waiting for someone to tell me never again and thus to sever the circle of repetitions and mistakes or to tell me you will find what you are seeking, knowing then that the object we're delving for doesn't have the face of a person or of evasion but of the final God and anyway we've dug so much under the planks of one floor after another, crack by crack, looking for a needle to unite us even if not in the same seam till we can follow the line of an invisible horizon and prove that the floor could be the ceiling especially when you roll face-up, face-down across the corrugated roof of the grain shed because you have to reach the rain gutter masterfully without falling over the other side in a race that Laura always wins while I'm always the little girl left behind by the dizziness upward overturned by the dizziness downward and by my terrible fear of the void not of the solitude I chose so as not to reconcile patience and adventure, not to be you and I in lukewarm encounters on the plank that stretches across the water tank from the front of one house to the other so they can join to form several rooms under my forehead to hold the wind and weather through which I move holding the hand of Aunt Adelaida who was a bulrush and who's going to take me to the amusement park with a different fiancé who ends up dying so she'll have to keep him with his dress suit in the glass case and scratch the initials off the rings but they don't know this yet so they let me drink beer until I start to see the light of the sparklers spinning round from the alcohol that feeds every nostalgia with the sky that stretches from nightfall to dawn and projects the light onto this wall where the Chinese shadows merge with animal heads that infect me every time my brother Alejandro takes me to the zoo and I can't seem to cut them out of the limits of my own head with its little angel crown on procession days or its headdress of black feathers brushing against this other wall that doesn't protect me from apparitions but rather allows every disappearance and against which I'll manage to cry for centuries, learning to mix the perverse and revealing intentions of each image and knowing in the end that I believe less and less in what I see as long as no one interrupts me until I understand that it's already too late to hang a pair of men's pants and one of my skirts repeated infinitely on the same hanger in this wardrobe that should be full of little damp handkerchiefs wrung dry from so much despair in the same meaningless monogram which is an imposter from start to finish but which nevertheless begins with the first letter of a name that I know will melt into the whole alphabet to give it some meaning, but that until now is the same name they use for calling me to go swing in the garden or to tell me about the great misfortunes or to threaten me with goblins at siesta time, or so I'm the one who says nevermore three times before the cock crows, rejecting any semblance of proximity to happiness because I still believe in the desperate conjunction of sun and moon over the earth over the terrace where I lay out the Tarot and the Hanged Man card appears, deciphered so many times for others who are undoubtedly so many of my other selves, with the relentlessness of a clock that morning after morning forces me to answer every knock, even when I sense there's no one there, unless we're all falling toward the abyss of the same sky.

"Mama, Papa," I cry out, falling. I can see the two faces appearing at the edge of total darkness.

One moves forward like a ship's prow, proof of everything that leaves, wrapped in an aura of unrecoverable losses, carved by knives made for engraving faith, blurry behind the particles of shadow into which the moon breaks at twenty-four, at twenty-eight, at thirty-six years of age. But my mother is not my mother: she's the unknowing seed of me.

The other face flees like a ship sailing away, proof of all that stays, wrapped in an aura of unreachable things, carved by knives made to break faith, blurry behind the particles of light into which the sun breaks at twenty-four, at twenty-eight, at thirty-six years of age. But my father is not my father: he's the unknowing seed of other men.

Inside this well, I'm spinning like the earth. Something sucks me upward. I rise. Mama, Papa, me: a splendid eclipse spreading over the hope of a race.

And Still the Wheel

. . .

The departure is irrevocable, as if we were moving inside a wheel, although we're on horseback. Galloping on a white horse, from Telén to Toay. For me it's like riding on the back of a stormy wind, and although I know the horse can't escape the wheel's circle, I hold on desperately to Grandpa Damián's poncho.

We left as evening fell, in the hour when sadness descends like a huge bird from the blue to the gray, scattering handfuls of ash, covering the entire plain in its death throes and not letting the advancing day pass, the day that could be escaping behind me, beneath those slowly closing wings.

I don't know. I swore I wouldn't turn my head so that nothing could make us go back to Telén. I can't look to the side either, because the house will reappear again and I might be sucked back into the rooms that smell of no escape. Those rooms where the dark furniture peers hungrily out of keyholes, where fleshy plants swell up imperceptibly among the shadows and lamps lower a yellow eyelid to hide what can't be seen.

I told myself Aunt Valeria might still be there on the other side of the gate, waving a useless handkerchief that doesn't even help her cry. Maybe she's still there, gazing distractedly, doing nothing but turning pale, and maybe it's already nighttime, I tell myself.

"Goodbye, Aunt Valeria. You're going to be stuck forever among smoky windows, as in an eclipse. It doesn't matter—they'll see you anyway. All the drawers in the house are spying on you so they can devour you and the plants suck you dry while you sleep, and in every corner there's a hooded figure with glowing eyes making the sign of the Bengal tiger. Goodbye, Aunt Valeria. You have the cold hands of a widow caressing flocks of black hens. It doesn't matter. I still love you, even if your voice stretches away so remotely that it floats on the air like the black crepe of someone else's mourning. I love you because your name would be Valeria even on the moon, because for three days you didn't spy on me to see me crying and because I know that you know that I know. Goodbye, Aunt Valeria: we'll never see each other again." Years later I'll see your last photograph, and you'll grow ever paler among the even fleshier plants, with your face that knows that I know that Alejandro is dead.

And I do know it. When the others think you don't know, they exchange glances of such exaggerated complicity that any fool would catch on, or maybe that's just why they do it—just to play the temptation game, and when they suspect you're suspicious, they sniff around anxiously as if there were a dead dog in some corner, all the while chatting glibly about the delightful smells of the season. When they know that you already know—like Valeria did—they join the common effort to be stubborn and indifferent witnesses to "that thing" that no one can whisk out of sight, because it already happened, and so will keep happening, even if it's forgotten. I know this. It's pointless for Grandpa Damián to have brought me here three days ago, supposedly "beforehand," pointless for him to take me home to Toay now, right on schedule, at the agreed-upon time, among the portents of nightfall and storm, as if it were only a matter of escaping the wind, as if meanwhile the wind had passed through my house, slamming shut the door that, when we get back, we'll find shut forever. I know it was much more than the wind, much more than a door. It was an abyss that for the first time they haven't let me cross along with the others. They dug it deeper for me during those three days of two absences, not knowing this death would infect me from any distance and would never leave me.

How did I find out, and when? I discovered it like so many other things, trying so hard until I couldn't see at all any longer, or trying to see backwards. I don't really know how the game is played, because once I get infected I can't start over again without knowing. I got the portrait of death ten days ago. I looked at it in order to test it, and kept looking until my gaze dizzied itself or sank beneath the surface of the water or moved to the edge of the flame, and then, in that image that had become the picture of a tremor or a shiver, though still motionless, my brother Alejandro's face appeared. I closed my eyes, and with my closed eyes I saw him with his eyes closed. His cheeks were more sunken, the lips paler—a sad color, a color that won't ever turn back to any other color, but instead will disappear deeper and deeper into that same color. And then I forgot it, until Grandpa Damián came and took me away to Telén three days ago, and I didn't ask, since I knew the face that transported us was that face, the one that kept spinning in the wheels of the carriage with its color of no return. I knew that's what being dead was, even if I knew nothing else. Nothing else that infected me until now, because ever since that time I can feel beneath my eyelids other closed lids that no force or sudden scare could ever raise again. Moving in its current, my blood drags along another motionless blood, heavy as a stone that keeps tugging downward until my blood, too, is made of stone; my heart beats over a heart forever paralyzed by the frost. Even now, it's chilling my tears.

We've come to a stop. Grandpa Damián dismounts and ties the horse to a post. I press my fists against my eyes so he'll believe I'm just sleepy. When I look again—and now I can look to the sides because I know that nothing will stop the wheel that carries us back without the carriage—he's already inside the store, inside the breathless blue cold that's lit by two kerosene lamps. He is timeless. As distant or as close as a tree, all depending on the protection or the abandonment you find in silence. Like the trees, he's made of a substance that is proud, impassive, deliberate, pensive, and sleepless. He is "Grandpa Damián" and not just simply "Grandpa," simply because he's not my mother's father but her uncle. For others he's just "Grandpa," but that doesn't make him any less of a tree, especially at night, when he and the trees seclude themselves in their patriarchal domain, in that slightly shadowy mystery that from the outside looks like a dream, but which must be the tool that carves Grandpa

Damián and the trees, and that keeps them from sleeping. Like now, when he walks up to me (though it always seems like it's me who moves toward him) and holds out a little package that looks not like a present but like something left for anyone on the branch of a tree, and he unties the horse and swings up onto it.

And we're spinning again on a spoke of the wheel; in the very center of the hub is Alejandro's face. Galloping again. But I'm no longer afraid of the beasts the night weaves behind my back, nor of the unthinkable hand that reaches out to grab me, because Grandpa Damián has put me in front of him in the saddle, and he's protecting my back with his body and my sides with the barrier formed by his arms and the reins that encircle me. Who told him I was afraid?

From now on, I'll discover any shape the road might take in the very same moment he does. I'm always less afraid of what I face with my own eyes than of what can surprise me, unforeseen. That's why I sleep with my back pressed to the wall, and why I can't sit down unless I'm facing an open door. Even if I don't hear anything, there can be balls of wool that mean something else, and they fall, bounce, and slip away silently; even if I see nothing, someone is weaving something against me. Of course everything's so dark now that it's almost as if it were happening backwards, as if that backwards were the whole night tangling up to envelop us. I feel the night working close at hand, crouched among the shivering brambles that alternately spread out and draw together around the edge of the open but impenetrable plain against the darkening sky. I can feel it gathering all its materials, dissolving those distant pale glimmers that suddenly show themselves like a kind of salvation and then sucking them into its own substance, into its skeins of horror. I feel it spreading out the taut fabrics on either side that it will tighten around us. I try not to look down so I won't see the weft and warp of that thing that was the road and that still propels us forward, but that at any moment might suddenly close up from underneath and behind, trapping us in the sack when we least expect it... If I look I slip, I fall inside and downward, I fall like a cold stone into the pit of the stomach, who knows how deep, if I can't manage to latch onto something from the outside. I lean forward and grip the horse's mane with both hands. I wish I could attach myself to him, get inside him through his skin, if only he'd let me. In my true condition I would walk on four feet or more. They've put me on two so they can measure me against a world I don't belong to, a world that runs a different race, that slips backward fastened to the innermost edge of my organism, unrolling me from this wheel of emptiness that spins like a whirling dervish at my very center. Wasn't I talking about weaving? They're unraveling me, winding up my skein of mystery, undoing me from the weft I thought I was woven into until the very end, and the great hollow of the wheel grows dizzily inside me, eating up my supports with a taste like powdery gray, like swollen wind, like the vomit of a fast. I can't understand the substance being drained from me, I can't absorb the spinning nausea that takes its place. If I throw myself from the horse right now, the substance that leaves me will spring back inside me like elastic, it will fill up the nausea and I'll shatter into a thousand pieces. If I stay on the horse, it will keep going ahead backwards, and the wheel of nausea, after hitting bottom, will toss my hollow shell against one of the walls of the universe. Why are they turning me inside out? And when will it stop?

The horse shakes its head, whinnies, slows down. Grandpa Damián's arm tightens around my waist and his hand pulls my head back, holding it hard against his belly. We stop. He dismounts and lifts me off. My legs tremble all the way up to my head. It's a vibration rising in tiny electric shocks, a bitter dizziness that corrodes my bones, loosens my joints, collides with my height and turns me into a rag. Though I didn't feel the vibration go down, it rises again, and will keep rising my entire life, crashing against the sum of all my years.

I drop to the parched earth and sit crying. The measure of my tears is the measure of the strength I regain, the awareness of my helplessness, a reincorporation into the resistant wall. Resisting what? Resisting something that seeks me out and that I half reject, something I want to explore without actually admitting it, but that won't let me in unless I detach myself entirely from my own entrails and abandon myself to its strength, without calling on any of my powers.

Grandpa Damián crouches by my side, caresses my head, and murmurs simply "Poor thing." If he says anything else, it's something that merges with my own voice and my own thoughts and I can't tell them apart. Just "Poor thing, poor thing," and nothing else. The same loneliness as being with God, with God who is fragmented so He can act with my acts and feel with my feelings, whose oneness suffers with my desecrations and grows with my love. An impartial witness for the duration of an inevitable journey among nightmares, to the end of time. We could stay here until then, until we're buried in this sand that starts to lift and spin, more and more, faster and faster.

Now we're on horseback again. We're moving forward slowly against the wind, almost sideways among the thirsty dust devils. It's going to rain. These thousand mouths that blow their desolate breath in every direction are crying out for rain. Then all at once they fall silent, amazed at the lightning's sudden threat. It dies away and flares up again, furious, menacing. Even if I keep believing the opposite, it's not the brightness of a door that opens, closes, and opens all at once so I can glimpse some unknown interior, something surprising whose very brilliance blinds us. It's not a miracle momentarily granted. No: it's the watchman in the high towers with his warning signal, it's the gleam of weapons prepared for annihilation. It tumbles all the way down the stairs. By the light of that lightning I stare at the candies Grandpa Damián gave me—as if he were leaving them on a branch—the first time we stopped, and I've squeezed them tightly in my fist this whole time, not noticing that the paper is torn, that it's candy and that my hand is sticky. They're perfect little opaque stones, pink, blue, and gray, with all the same imperfections, indentations, and highlights of any little stone or talisman you might hold onto in order to not feel alone or to look at in the light and remember. Maybe these little stones are for not remembering. They're probably sweet but sad, like any memory that's savored before being forgotten. They're a bribe for my grief and my fear. I consider them in their lowliness in a different light and with infinite compassion, with a pity like crystallized honey that hurts my throat. They look as woebegone as I do. Because I've never found in this world any object to exchange for my grief or my fear. Any coin traded would increase them, changing its value immediately, taking on the price of my compassion at the cost of my helplessness, even when that coin is engraved with the effigy of calamity. Fraud, vengeance, bitterness—they bought nothing in me but a territory of compassion where the thickets of another grief and another fear grow wild, sheltered by my own lack of shelter. I establish those realms with these dark and insoluble stones, the opaque one, the pink, the light blue, and the gray. On them I build the dwelling of my strength and my defects, while the sand lashes my cheeks relentlessly.

The horse neighs, rears up, shakes its head nervously, refuses to go on. Something is coming close. Something comes rolling down the road without any wheel. Between two winks of lightning I can just make out a shadowy shape. It's a huge, brownish, spiny figure, made of air and aggression. It comes closer, light and unsteady, lacking skin or heart, and thus apparently lacking mystery. But it belongs to the world of unfathomable, outward repetition, to the world of unintentional and blind threat—maybe the most dangerous kind, since the most forceful denial operates everywhere, but invisibly. I wonder from what distance it orders this messenger of fate to reach out of the void, to envelop and incorporate us like water, shadow, or stain. Let it come then, let it invade us, let it change us into another appendage identical to the rest of its stiff nothingness. Horse, old man, and child: we'll keep moving inside another wheel of uncontrolled and irreversible fate, whose center will continue to spin simply with the hands of the clock, until the absurd universe is absurdly consummated. But no. It brushes past us and goes on its way. And so it will grow in its aridity, gathering other identical shapes into its outsized bulk, other shapes equally uprooted and directionless. I have known atrocious moments that look exactly like this thing.

Grandpa Damián says simply: "That was a tumbleweed."

And horse, old man, and child, we'll continue on our irrevocable journey fashioned of silence, penury, and obstinacy. And what if we were moving inside another wheel just like this one? No, it couldn't be the same, since wherever we go, at the end of all weakness and all tenacity, stands the house. It's inside my eyes and it shines in the stormy darkness of distance like a jewel, like an ember, like a phosphorescent diamond. I know that in one of the facets of that jewel an opaque lightning bolt bursts forth, I know that one of the walls of that house already has a crack where it will begin to crumble. I try not to look at that face misted over by the death of the face that transports us: I try to imagine my back against the wound of the wall that bleeds us dry. I just want to see luminous heads gathered around the lamps without counting how many there are, I want to feel the gentle rub of the warm sheets, without thinking about those growing colder in a bed no one will ever unmake, I want to smell the scent of wood inside and the scent of sweetened lemon wafting in from outside without searching below for the trace of lavender that will gradually dissipate, absorbed by damp handkerchiefs—the smell that might already be gone. But I can't erase it, because that scent is Alejandro and it's Alejandro who carries me, who plunges me into stillness, who pins me like a butterfly beneath the frost of his heart.

It's impossible to breathe inside that motionless cold. I can't absorb the frozen mask that tightens over my face. Everything has stopped. I inhabit the mummy that is the world. They've embalmed the air and the landscape that I can't see. Maybe they've embalmed Grandpa Damián and the horse too, in the up and down of this endless carousel. If only something around us would move, even a rope across the road... I'd choose the stinging of the sand in the lashing wind over this paralysis that plugs up my nose and ears. It's an unbearable suspense, an empty bowl that no one knows how to fill. But no, they're filling it now. Great drops of rain have begun to fall against my maskless face, against the greedy earth. I can't see the ground but I imagine it absorbing the drops, holding them intact, hiding them like a miser. They're coming down faster now, more insistent; the ground strives to hide them quickly in its deepest creases and corners. A thousand years from now they could dig down and find that buried rain, and I'd tell them how it came to be. Maybe in that time all my fears, my vertigo, Grandpa Damián, the tumbleweed, the horse, and the insoluble stones will still be alive—will all be witnesses of this interminable journey. Each one will be able to claim for itself a portion of relief when they parcel it out. I breathe deeply, inhaling the water-woven air.

Grandpa Damián covers my head and wraps his poncho around me almost twice. *It was in those days that the grandfather returned from Vercelli with the dead woman.* This is a sign. The response is immediate: lightning, thunder, and the vein traced by the bolt that's going to fall, that's falling now. The poncho is white, and the horse too; all we need is a mirror for the lightning to see itself. We'll draw the lightning toward us. We're crying out to it with all this white that seems to reject everything but in reality attracts all the worst. White is the herald of catastrophes; black pronounces them gone. We will cross from one to the other, from this opaque ice to coal. We'll stay intact, changed only into our own mourning (oh, how the black crepe of your voice will change, Aunt Valeria!), into the statues of our own grief. I know because I've heard it: the one who killed his brothers and made off with the treasure in a white sheet, the veiled bride who fled through the fields, and the saint's tunic that got caught on the mimosa: all were the black witnesses of their own punishment. But why should we be punished? Because of the future, of course, because of all weakness and renunciation, all extreme patience, and because of their counterparts, obstinacy and pride, ever present through all the years to come and that made this journey possible when I was only five years old. Punishment plunges me into whole decades anticipated by the wheel, forcing me to take part in a memorial to somber wanderings, until those decades truly pass and I'm reduced to a little pile of dull ash from which anyone could blow away each particle of stubbornness and pride. Even so, after endless revolutions of the wheel in limitless time, the particles will come together again, animated by weakness, sacrifice, and infinite patience, so that I may continue the journey, since I've got to get home one way or the other.

But the bolt doesn't fall. It has gone back inside those doors that the lightning is opening and closing. And there above, doors and walls are crashing against each other, holding the lightning back. It's a noisy and dazzling battle behind a thickness of water that won't let me see.

"No, not here!" I shout—because I've just seen it.

"We've got no choice. There's no other road," the voice of God responds, the voice of Grandpa Damián. And we gallop faster, and his arm holds me tighter.

I just saw it. In the light of the vein that touched the roots of the earth, I just saw, engraved in the mist by the gaze of the rain, the cupolas with their suddenly lighted crosses that appear over the top of the wall, and above the main gate the irremediable angel that calls to us. I ask God, I ask Grandpa Damián, "Did we need this cruelty too?" "We've got no choice, there's no other road," he answers, they answer. No. There's no other road to get to Alejandro, to his eyes the color of green silk behind yellow flames, to the empty hands of that young and modest champion of all the games. But now, Alejandro's eyes are an acid where every portrait in the world is submerged and erased, and his hands hold nothing but the menacing banner of a motionless victory over time. No, there's no other road any more. On the outside, it's a terrifying funnel sucking me down from the chill of my hair so it can drag me into an assembly of nameless bones presided over by that woman who can wear all the faces in the world. And on the inside, it's an endless slope down which I tumble under my foaming blood that continues to live among the dead.

"Alejandro: this isn't just one of your games, is it? If it were, I wouldn't mind following you because I know we're like the continuation of a single color, and no color belonging to anyone else will ever be able to dye us to look different. To be alone with you, wherever that may be, is a testimony to a prior ramification, no matter what trials they submit us to. The mystery begins and possibly ends the same way, and maybe you already know it. But this isn't a game we both play: it's you plotting against me. Are you making pacts outside our clan?"

"It's not true, he's not there," I tell myself, closing my eyes so what I say will be true.

I organize my terror without Alejandro. I materialize it in those small enclosed spaces of the Day of the Dead, where all objects are useless and yet appear recently touched by someone who just hid himself, just dissolved into that tense, pervaded, almost organic air, because it's only in the rarefied deposit, the formless body where the molecules of invisibility remain suspended. Those particles constantly seek each other out; they're probably looking for each other right now to recover their cohesion in an easy effort of memory. They don't even seek, they simply attract each other. They, the dead, remake themselves. Because just like each substance here contains a part that struggles to fall, condemned to death, in that place, too, every substance must have a part that struggles to raise itself, condemned to life. This mixture of forces in a single substance disturbs me, and yet it's inside me, in my own seed, in the origin of the corpse that I will be.

Since birth I've been locked in with my own enemy, unknown to me. Now that they're getting nearer, I only ask that he not make pacts with them, with those like him. They are dense transparencies, armies wrought in rarefied clouds of smoke, vibrating windgusts ready for any metamorphosis. And there in front is the woman with her flower-fringed hat and her jaws strong from chewing butterflies. I don't want to think about the dampness of those flowers or the crunching of the butterflies. Or the blurred faces that are coming this way. It's a cold and foggy tide, with circular waves like those of moiré silk. There it is. It rises up and freezes us, its tightening circles trapping us inside. They fasten themselves in blue streaks from the feet up to the throat: the marble absorbs us. This light is the last streak, the bright bandage that covers our eyes forever. I shout at the very moment when the bolt stuns us. I hear myself howl in the din of the sky that tilts down and severs the flagstones and drags us into the plummeting columns that held up the vault of the immense cathedral. They uproot us from the world of the living and tumble us down with the dead. I am an endless moaning that turns me inside out, descends with me to the subsoil. It's going to fall suddenly silent with the stone door that will extinguish the light on my face. My final appearance is this well, opened by my own cry—and they're going to close me up.

"Blessed Saint Geronimo, Sweet Saint Barbara!" says Grandpa Damián, almost in a whisper, breaking the expected fall, turning the well right side up, making my ears appear again. "It struck over by the church."

The damp breath that snuffs out my face brings me back from the depths. We are incredibly in the present. And then I see again—as if through a glass where all the world's weeping is condensed—the ragged night, still upright over the earth, with its suit of wintry vapors, its old garland of yellow lights torn to shreds. It's coming toward us across the plaza: dripping water, it leaps over the hedges. I'd also like to run holding night's hand, disheveled and barefoot over the immortal ground.

But I'm still tied to the wheel that carries us, and maybe I've forgotten how to walk. Wrapped in the poncho that smells of wild weather, crossing the blurred strata of heat and cold, I've been reduced to a miserable larva, stuck not to memory or to the promise of sun, but simply to the effort to breathe, to contract and expand the pitiful ration of air that sustains me. Shaken for who knows how long by the intermittent echo of the sob that was left buried inside me, I can barely manage this breath. I toss it out in little pieces, in a kind of smothered hiccup, all along the length of the Larrain estate.

And there is our house, darkened, encased in its mourning.

When Grandpa Damián lowers me to the ground, I feel that I have no beginning or end, no hands or feet, I'm an undifferentiated sameness of chill and fever, still disoriented by the impulse of the wheel that spins unevenly now in some empty place in my chest. Maybe the wheel will stop and I'll collapse over the void like a rag. But no. I'm still the wrapping of the sobs that haven't stopped spilling out. Maybe I've dug down all the way to the last day of my life, because it keeps happening even when I see my sister María de las Nieves sitting in the hallway, pale and dressed in black, and when I hear her say from so far away, as if she were speaking forever:

"Alejandro went away. Three days ago Elijah came for him in his chariot of fire and they went up to the sky. Just now, when the lightning hit, it looked like a chariot wheel and I thought they were coming back. I lifted up my feet, and it rolled under me and fell into the cistern."

Then the wheel of the journey, the wheel of fire, passes over me, over Alejandro's face, over the sobs that won't stop. And it still rolls on.

Nanni Sometimes Flies

. . .

Nanni used to sing in the grain shed. Every dawn he would appear in the imaginary setting of the forest he had lost once and for all. It was as if he kept the forest embalmed in some inevitable nook of his dreams and would grab it as he came out, furtively, with his dissembling air of a pickpocket of weeds, a vanisher of frogs and hares.

The truth is that his forest was brought to life each morning in our granary. If not, what was that chaos of cries and murmurs, those hurried trots and flutterings that burst forth after a long yawn, in an endless crescendo like a message being sent toward the most distant ear? Wasn't it the stifling of all the members of the choir who struggled to tear themselves completely out of their lethargic tapestry? And couldn't that victorious shrillness have been the chant that arose from the revelation of green, from the forest's true voice recently resurrected in all its glory? Yet the true voice of the green came from the birds and was lifted to the sky in a boundless and overwhelming chirping.

Nanni would sing. The birds would sing. They took turns rehearsing surprise, greeting, nostalgia, fear, and joy in an infinite range from high-pitched to low, made of repetitions, alternations, and stubborn insistences prolonged to breath's exhaustion.

Then came the gargling. It was the moment when all the throats of the forest trembled hoarsely in unison, shaken by the gurgling of the waters. It was suspense and the premonition of something miraculous.

Then the gentleman appeared in the luminous clearing and ardently intoned his familiar song.

It wasn't hard to imagine him in front of the iron stand that held the blue washbasin decorated with tiny bouquets of forget-me-nots with lilac-colored bows. Standing and holding in one hand the glass from whose blue depths a few trapped bubbles escaped upwards, he would examine in the fragment of mirror on the wall, the arid plains of his skin crossed by a mercurial groove like a dry river. His small eyes, burned-out coals where a deep spark moved restlessly or hid itself willfully among the ashes, would keep a suspicious watch over that stranger, over that intruder who had taken possession of his face overnight. His eyes would try in vain to catch him unawares in a careless or relaxed moment. Then his bony hand would move up to his forehead, entering the mirror with life of its own, almost unrecognizable. He would see it act of its own accord, digging with little jerky movements under his bangs, then jumping to the chin where it anxiously fingered the sparse tangle, looking for the suture line that would reveal the fraud, the usurper, the scar of the imposter. But there was nothing. Not even a tiny fray at the edge that would allow him to peel off the unbearable mask of the failed tenor, not even the faintest relief, the slightest indication that he might use for accusation and unmasking.

And there it was again, that raucous noise. The mirror thrown angrily aside, another piece broken off each day, as if by doing this it would slowly corrode the lie it reflected, as if the number of fragments were lessening that lie instead of multiplying it. And when the only thing left was a little pile of sharp-edged dust in which he couldn't even prove the fall of the despised imposter, then he'd detach those alien expressions one by one until the last one displaced wouldn't matter at all. The commotion of the crowd, the fervent bows, the applause, the narrow passage opened with great effort between two living walls of exaltation would be the irrefutable reflection, the true evidence of his true face.

All this he explained the day he arrived. I had made a mental note of that conversation I heard from my bed, but couldn't see. It came from the ivy, was carried by the stirring of the ivy up to the iron bars on my window. One tone was calm, inquiring. The other was urgent, hollow, secretive, anxious, interrupted suddenly by a squeaky, unexpected sound that surprised its very owner, that slowed him down and stopped him. Then there was a short pause until he untangled himself from that ascending metallic chord and repeated the previous tone.

"... I don't know, a vague memory, I can't be sure," said the conciliatory voice of my grandmother, who always found some sediment, some trace of explanation for everything.

"But of course, of course! It was in all the papers, in all the announcements, in all the magna cartas. It took place in the Sesame Forest. It was famous, Ma'am, famous."

"What did you say the name was?"

"Sesame. The Sesame Forest. All the sounds. Tutti quanti." He laughed from high to low, like a waterfall. "And the aria? Two thousand two hundred forty-seven, with ninety-nine people standing. Bravo! Bravo! Bravo!" The ascending metallic spiral had been interrupted again; it encircled him and pulled him upward. "I wave comically. Così. Calm and arrogant. Green coat, green shoes, green eyes. Green. Bravo. More green. More bravo. Greener than green. Bravissimo!" The ivy picked up all of his voice and threw it in torrents through my window. There was applause.

"Shhh! Enough—you'll wake everyone up. What did you say the name was?"

"How do I know? The whole cast. Andisco, Fittipaldi, Berardinelli, Palma, Andrani: birds. Sparrows, pitiful sparrows. Fittipaldi, Knight of the Forest: at your service! Green hat, blonde hair, blonde beard, blonde or strawberry blonde, green eyes."

"But—you?.... Blonde hair and green eyes? Really... And what did you say the name was?"

"What did you say? What did you say? What did you say that one's name was? What did you say?" He crooned softly, distractedly, to the tune of *Sulle Labbra*. "Fittipaldi, Señora. Fittipaldi. The two Fittipaldis: the knight of the forest and the extra. Fittipaldi the Great and the other Fittipaldi, the miserable swine. But look at my face. Do you think this used to be my face? This face is an insult—do you understand?" I heard a slapping sound and then an exclamation of reproach and surprise. "You have to squash it to see who's underneath, so everyone can see how many of us there are. No, no, ma'am. Blonde hair and green eyes. Two Fittipaldis—do you see what I mean? I'm going to tell you in confidence and discretely, as befits the high personages that govern our destinies. . . ." The ivy was releasing the voice, letting it drift away. (I could imagine the look of understanding, the calm but stubborn gesture with which my grandmother was taking this in.) All that reached me now, skipping from leaf to leaf, were a few loose words, a few syllables that didn't add up to anything—"the last time. . . he sang more. . . he, he, he. . . trilogy. . . . . . surpation. . . ture. . . unhappy. . . such. . . ." And then just the ivy fluttering against the iron bars.

None of that meant anything until days later. When I saw him leaning against the doorframe in the kitchen—a startling apparition in the moment when I appeared, a pale mannequin snatched from the store window of some nightmare—with his impeccably white tennis shoes, his costume pants, the rat-black frock coat with velvet edging and the top hat with a verdigris rosette on the band, it still meant nothing. Nor did it begin to mean anything when I looked straight into his face: his damp black hair, lavishly spread over his forehead forming bangs that looked like mine, except that in his, all the fierce teeth of the comb left their mark; his small and jittery eyes that flashed on and off, the fleeting little lights that burned in their depths while the eyes themselves remained transfixed, veiled, dark; the skin of his cheeks like a bird's skin trying to stick to a bone that was too sunken, cheeks mottled by the threat of feathers that struggled to sprout despite the boiling water; and below all that, the straight, thick hairs of a sparse, narrow, stunted beard that grew reluctantly and abashedly.

But even if it still held no meaning, that conversation I had tucked away became suddenly illuminated, showing me its two sides: one indecipherable, engraved with cryptographic characters meant for those who ask What for? and the other accessible, with figures joined by a line pointing to the exit, meant for those who ask Why? I sensed that by following the outline of the first one, of the face turned toward my grandmother (in spite of who she was), the paths opened, multiplied, overlapped, taking me away from the forest clearing I needed to reach. But in the warp and weft of the second side, the side that was turned toward the little man, I could already see the golden thread that would lead me directly to the place where Sesame would open in the foliage, revealing to me the mystery of the two Fittipaldis, of the knight and of the verdure.

He took off his hat and stepped toward us, bending forward in a confident bow.

"Good morning, Princesses," he said smiling, and an eyelid descended quickly, extinguishing one of the little lights.

"Good morning," answered Laura with an identical gesture, as if she knew the ritual by heart.

"The Queen Mother, your grandmother, has given me lodging in the granary, next to the carriage-house, and your father, the morganatic gentleman, has given me a chest filled with fancy attire, as well as some allusive documents. I've selected this finery to maintain the disguise that is proper to my lymphatic nature, without spoiling the elegance that governs the institutions in power." All the while the little lights flickered quickly on and off, but the speech was brilliant and was delivered unhesitatingly.

"Will you be staying long?" asked Laura, who worried that the granary, one of her favorite places, would be occupied.

"It all depends. Maybe, maybe not. Or who knows. . . ." Once again he stopped. He threw his head back as if following with his eyes the chirping of the voice that had ascended in a long tin-foil cone. "May I invite you to take a stroll, if that doesn't violate the rules of three-times-four?" And we set off walking.

"I know up to my fives!" I exclaimed proudly, thinking of the multiplication tables.

"I know them all," said Laura, and she hummed the monotonous little ditty every school child knows.

"Very good, very good! Careful not to ruin that voice, because the voice is one of the signs of wisdom, as it's been called. The sign is raised: they stop and then they answer. The sign is lowered: everyone passes and no one answers. The red light comes on: watch out, warning, it's about to start. The green light comes on. . . ."

"And you appear!" I said, thinking of that morning's conversation.

He stopped, disconcerted.

"Bravo, bravo, Princess." He stood in front of me and took my hands. His own were damp and trembled slightly. He brought his little lights close to my face and looked intently into me. He smelled like a wet dog and I wanted to cry. "Ah. . . you know." And he let me go. We started walking again. "Bravo: I appear."

"Where?" asked Laura who was walking backwards in front of us.

"In the Sesame Forest," he replied impatiently, as if it were the obvious answer, but right away he smiled and produced a nightingale from his throat.

"As in, 'Open, Sesame'? But that's a cave," protested Laura absent-mindedly, looking backwards so she didn't trip.

"Forest. An entirely green forest. All the wild animals, the wind, the town of Milan. I make my appearance." He stooped down, picked up a bone that looked like a butterfly skeleton, scrutinized it exhaustively from every angle, then put it in his pocket.

"A cave. Just ask my grandmother," Laura insisted. She was doing little jumps, crossing her feet back and forth. Her skinny legs covered with long red woolen tights looked like the double feathers of a scissortail. If scissortails were red. "The cave of the forty thieves. Ali Baba comes and says 'Open, Sesame!'"

"Forty thieves? One thief, just one thief!" he almost howled, shaking his index finger furiously. Then he burst into laughter that suddenly sharpened and rose up and broke like a long needle of frost.

"Forty thieves. Ali Baba arrives and says, 'Open, Sesame,'" Laura repeated stubbornly, glancing backwards from the height of her little jump.

"I arrive—I or no one. Fittipaldi, Knight of the Forest. Green coat, green shoes, green eyes."

We stopped. We had reached the door of the shed.

"Green eyes?" we both exclaimed at the same time. My voice sounded nervous, and for the first time I heard in Laura's voice a distrustful and mocking tone.

"That's right. Green eyes."

We went into the shed. The granary was up above. The three of us sat down on the stairs. In the middle, one step or branch above, the large, dark, unseemly bird, faded from harsh rains; to the right, the red scissortail; to the left, the blue scissortail that was me. Three birds stiff with cold in the frozen shade of the branches, breathing in the smell of dusty sacks in storage, the smell of enclosure, of risky adventures that always ended in punishment. Three birds waiting for some mysterious spell that would turn us into something else, or for some trail of grains that would lead us from the crossroads over some unforeseen distance to a pair of green eyes that watched us from an irretrievable face. But then the discolored rook took off with a single wing-flap down a twisted path that he alone knew and down which Laura and I could barely advance step by step, in spite of our long bird legs made for great leaps and our high-flying bird ways.

"The little princess knows. I'm going to tell you in confidence and secretly, or rather, with great care. It was the last time I sang; it was the first time I sang with this face, without my signature. Adesso, adesso, adesso," he said mournfully. The metallic coil had sprung loose again and nothing could stop it now.

We were moving down a dilapidated path. No recognizable seed for our growing hunger. They must have all been devoured by our guide in his endless migrations. But that didn't matter. The path was woven on the face of the fabric that showed on our side, and the bright thread that got tangled, ran and returned, would finally carry us to our destiny if we were patient enough to follow it through many days in its myriad evolutions within the labyrinth. I counted on it. That's how I managed to find, among snarls of innocence and knots of raving, the line of a drawing that illustrated a story of triumph and imposture: two identical names, one destiny of triumph and another of failure—that of the noble gentleman and great tenor, and that of the obscure stand-in—switched by virtue of two faces transformed ("reciprocally," he insisted) overnight, an apparently unnoticed exchange. And who would hear the protest?

The aggrieved party hurries to the theater on the night of the ill-fated day. He finds his dressing room occupied. Nevertheless, he's not discouraged. He joins the team of forest sounds and sings backstage like the obscure, almost anonymous Fittipaldi. But in the moment when the false knight appears, he breaks onto the stage and disputes with him the major aria; he seizes it from the other by right, by mutual understanding. (The one between him and the aria. He spoke of the aria like a woman who chooses from two suitors her true and rightful love; he spoke of it like a blind woman whom instinct could not fool and who was also the only witness, before God and eternity, to that incredible deception.) And the aria was not mistaken. She followed him submissively, of her own free will, until the bandits came and seized him by the limbs and threw him out of the place, amid the cheers and applause of the crowd, which in spite of its enthusiasm fails to intervene in his favor, because he can't cross over, can't leap over the abyss that separates one time from another. There are rules, and such a thing is prohibited. The public merely acknowledges him from the other side of the pit, while he, forever a prisoner of that denouement, hurls from the air his accusation and his curse, which no one can hear. This spectacular exit became confused in his memory with an exit from his own life. From that moment he loses his title, his possessions, his family, and enters handcuffed into "an amusement park for forgetting." But he can't forget. He doesn't want to forget. He'd rather resurrect the forest each morning, uproot it from that corner of sleep where it lies embalmed, lost once and for all.

After the gargling, after the great torrents of water, comes the aria. Now. The voice rises clear, precise, majestic, like the ascension of an angel. It breaks off, starts over. No. Once again. This is the point where life halts. Let it fly, let it lift up and glide horizontally above the green treetops. But no. It flutters, it flutters in place, unable to keep its balance. It falls, completely broken. The dazzling angel falls from its height, turned into a rook. Silence. It's the moment when they carry him offstage all over again.

When he left unexpectedly many months later, I found a little piece of mirror in the granary, along with a broken comb and two half-carved bones: in one I could just make out a devil, with his too-familiar traits; in the other I could imagine an angel, its wings still shackled.

There was also a clipping from a newspaper, carefully folded. He must have dropped it as he went out—I don't think he would have left it intentionally. It was a group photograph, faded and worn, from a gathering of opera fans in Viareggio. With a couple of pencil-strokes, a clumsy hand had changed the main actor's face, adding a scrubby and pitiful beard.

In the background, a furious "X" mercilessly cancelled out the anonymity of another face.

Dwarves

. . .

"I don't want it. It's got eyes," said Laura once again.

"It's got eyes," I echoed her half-heartedly.

"Chicken eyes," added Laura.

"Like Blindman's Bluff for chickens? Blind Chicken's Bluff!" I chimed in eagerly, sensing a game.

Laura touched my foot under the table. I understood. Any secret sign marked the beginning of her authority and of my submission. Something was about to begin and I, as always, had to follow her orders.

She looked at María de las Nieves who, in the absence of all the adults, presided over the table with the startling dignity of her sixteen years. At this point Laura smiled, puckered her lips, and shoving her chin forward in a funny kind of skunk-face—that weird twisted grimace that made any solemnity impossible, the face that later would make them erase her from all the photographs—began to enunciate rapidly, in her half-defiant, half-amused tone:

"Bull's eye, eye of the hurricane, eyes of a butchered lamb, eye of a keyhole, out of sight, out of mind; an eye for an eye, a tooth for a tooth; eye, eye . . ." and she ran out of ideas. The first words had resounded caustically, accusingly; the last were only a weak and uninspired outburst. She looked at me, egging me on.

"Eye see you," I said foolishly, by silly association.

But Laura loved it. Then, as if a password had been spoken, we launched unblinkingly, between giggles, into a dizzying litany, taking turns:

"I spy, I spy." "What do you spy?" "Eyes, eyes, eyes." "Turn a blind eye." "Look before you leap." "Feast your eyes on me." "The eye of God is upon you." "Stop, look, and listen." "Oh to see Rome and then to die..."

"Veni, vidi, vici!" shouted Nanni from the other side of the door with a sharp and victorious voice.

The voice stopped. We were quiet.

From the start, María de las Nieves had pounded slowly with her pale knuckles on the table, signaling her displeasure. This was only going to get worse: it would become a furious drum. We picked up our spoons.

The chicken soup remained untouched in our bowls. The large and small oily eyes floating on the surface were covered by now with a thin insulating film, whitish, like drops of suet. Now it was impossible to eat the soup. It almost made me feel sick.

The spoons were raiding the surface constantly, shifting around those disgusting eyes with their blind stare. But there they stayed, not rising to our mouths.

"I can't eat it," Laura complained. "It's made with melted candles."

"A candle for every saint," I said timidly, just in case we were still playing, just in case we might be able to keep this up until who knows when.

"Candle, candelabra, candescent, cancer, canary, don't burn the candle at both ends!" shouted María de las Nieves. The first five words had inspired us; we supposed that she wanted to be in the game with us. But no, this was no game. Her pale face got redder and redder, and her dark, almond eyes stretched closer and closer to her temples, sparking angrily like the gleam of weapons glimpsed through a thicket. "Idiots!" she added with teeth clenched as if to hold in another weapon: the most dangerous one. She opened her lips and slowly sucked in a mouthful of air, the paltry air that would be denied her years later, when, in order to reach her lungs, it had to pass through a zone of thick and corrupt vegetation, wrapped in suffocating emanations, like a jungle on a summer night.

"Idiots!" she repeated. For Laura and me, the fun had been stopped in its tracks, but our smiles stayed in place, embarrassed, unsure of how to disappear in a dignified way from our faces. "What do I care if you eat your soup or not! It's not true that it'll help you grow if you eat it. Enough stupid stories! It's not really true that it'll help you grow even if you do eat it. You're never going to grow, because you're dwarves. Real dwarves, both of you—and old ones too. Two stupid old dwarves, and it's time you realized it." She pushed back her chair, got up quickly, and walked out of the dining room with a majestic air that was beginning to hint at the permanent bearing of a great Roman lady.

She had hit us right between the eyes.

Laura and I exchanged glances like two stunned birds. Any gesture would have been a desperate wing-flutter, any word, an unbearably shrill screech. No—even if we were both the same, the revelation was too monstrous to begin sharing it.

Almost at the same moment we jumped out of our chairs and went running from the dining room through different doors. That's how it always happened. Significant moments always led us toward different doors. It was like that later, too: mine would take me toward that succession of doors that opened for a moment into the light, into open air, until others would appear, waiting like traps—those that inhaled me in order to enclose me alone with my desperate and almost pitiful destiny. But Laura's doors were few, and only opened onto a placid happiness.

This time I didn't take refuge under the oak tree. It was nighttime, and besides, I needed a shelter that would be timeless, permanent, maybe definitive. I lay face down on my bed and cried. I cried until I could feel the sand (from what arid, unknown depth did those sands always arise?) scratching my eyelids. It was only then that I began to think. Up to that point, I had only cried over my own wretched and unchanging little image of a dwarf condemned to dwarfhood.

I was a dwarf. I had only known two dwarves: Felicitas and Chico Dick. I had seen them in the circus, posted on either side of the entrance to the tent, with their red suits covered with fringes, gold trim and braids, their gleaming boots and helmets with black visors shading their tired and resentful eyes. My grandmother, who couldn't see very well, said "Good afternoon, children," as she walked by, stretching out her arms on either side to tweak their ears comically. But those angry faces that looked up at her, those tight-jawed faces with their hard and resolute expression, didn't look anything like children's faces. Or like our faces. It seemed like someone had worked hard to stuff the dwarves, pounding them down from the top, then squeezing on the sides to distribute the weight along their short bones. That operation had spoiled everything about them, making them swell under the eyes, in the wrists, and in other spots. Their steps were short and their vague movements, whose range was more limited than a child's, dragged their entire bodies about as if something were hindering them, or as if they had membranes or uncut stitching between their fingers and between their joints. They would tilt to one side and then the other, like very slowly spinning tops.

There were the other dwarves, too, magic ones, those that lived among mushrooms, lichen, and mosses that appeared suddenly in the deepest part of the forest, in those regions that take on a blood-red or saffron color when evening falls. But those dwarves were men and had white beards. No, that wasn't the case here.

I was a dwarf and an old dwarf at that. And yet I didn't have distant memories, or I just didn't know how to measure them backwards in order to determine my age. I didn't have trunks filled with objects, or outfits from the olden days, or knowledge of things that people spoke of as happening many years ago. Mama, Papa, my grandmother, María de las Nieves, Aunt Adelaida, Alejandro—whom I was told I wouldn't see until much later, unless I got a seat in Elijah's chariot (I thought Elijah must have a black moustache, bluish-purple skin covered with green tattoos, and a noisy little cart full of trinkets)—everyone, everyone was always the same. I hadn't seen them grow bigger or get old. Of course there was the family album with its serious portraits, and also the photos in which Laura showed me the white spots covering her sudden skunk-face, saying proudly, "I'm always the same, the one who changes least, and I'm the palest too." I recalled the photographs one by one. But that didn't shed light on anything. I didn't yet know the relentless prolixity of time. And yet, maybe dwarves forgot everything. On the other hand, I was now discovering the meaning behind so many other things: conversations cut short, pregnant pauses, concealed signs, sentences charged with mystery and allusion, and especially my mother's laughter when I asked her if I was there on the day she got married. But why had they repeated tiresomely, sometimes like a promise and sometimes like a threat: "When you grow up . . ."? No. I wouldn't be growing up. I couldn't be a saint, or a diver, or a horsewoman. Goodbye, brilliant and heroic destinies. Farewell sparkle of stained-glass windows illuminating my martyrdom and my saintly face raised toward the sky. Goodbye phosphorescences under the sea, white coral and sunken ships where there are always terrible secrets to discover. Goodbye spotlights, diaphanous dress spinning and spinning and spinning and white horse on which I'd balance on one foot as I made the victory lap.

I sobbed over all the snuffed out lights, all the little pieces of broken glass.

Someone took my hand, squeezed it affectionately and held it in her own. They were warm, small hands, belonging to the other dwarf.

I lifted my head a little and looked at her sidewise, slowly, though my damp hair. She didn't make me feel disgusted, or afraid, or apprehensive, only cared for and safe. Laura was sitting on the edge of the bed. She seemed almost calm, but pensive.

"I've got the whole story," she said in the low, sad voice she used for sharing any news. Births, visitors, even rainstorms became in her voice something threatened, completely vulnerable. "I asked María de las Nieves. She told me that many, many years ago, when our grandparents came to live in this house, there was a tree that later withered and died. In one of the lowest branches, which was still high because the tree was very tall, they found a nest with two white eggs. The eggs had little garlands with pink flowers like confectionary flowers and some letters that said *souvenir.* Around each one there was also a pink velvet band with a bow. They looked like Easter eggs, but they weren't. (María de las Nieves, in all her generosity, couldn't even grant us that.)

The circus was in town in those days, so our grandparents hired Felicitas and Chico Dick to sit on the eggs. After the dwarves climbed the tree, the ladder was removed so they couldn't get down. For forty days and forty nights they sat there on the nest in their hussar uniforms. (This coincidence with the forty days and nights of the Flood almost made Laura proud, as if all of us—nest, eggs and dwarves—had been brought over in the Ark.) From a distance they looked like two huge red birds, though they didn't sing. Every single day our grandparents took them whole platters of French fries and soup tureens full of chocolate mousse, and even dates and champagne. Then they'd take the ladder away again. During the day, Grandmother would sit at the foot of the tree and tell them children's stories, ghost stories, and even the lives of the saints. Sometimes Grandfather would play ball or guessing games with them. When they thought the dwarves' attention was wandering, Grandfather would poke them with the tip of his cane and Grandmother would shake her finger at them, so they would approach their task with more zeal. At night, after dinner, the band would come from town and play "The March of the Giants" (I couldn't fathom that show of hostility) until Felicitas and Chico Dick would fall asleep. On Sundays and holidays Father Indalecio would come and make them pray with him. Then he would climb up to a higher branch, ten yards or so above their heads, to give them the impression that he was standing in the pulpit, and from there he would preach to them. He looked like another bird, an enormous black bird that cawed and flapped its wings. Sometimes he would get excited about his sermon, about God's wrath about the sinners' punishment, and he would shake the tree limbs violently. When that happened, a rain of leaves and acorns fell on the two faces that were raised intently to him. One morning, the dwarves said it was finished, everything was ready and it was a job well done. When they came down from the tree, two little creatures could be seen in the nest: you and I, newborn babies. Since then, we've lived in this house. Later on, Mama was born, and then Aunt Adelaida and then everybody else."

Laura fell silent, her gaze fixed on the wall, lost in a daydream. So that was the story, the cruel, secret, humiliating story?

"I don't believe it!" I shouted. "That's impossible. Grandmother didn't recognize the eggs, and besides, why didn't they just let them rot? Why did they have to call Felicitas and Chico Dick? Why didn't they just put them with the hens' brood? Why? Why?" I pleaded hoarsely between sobs, hoping that Laura would have thought about it as much as I had, that she would have found something useful in all that mental review of family albums, memories, and people, and that she would offer it to me now as a possibility of salvation, even if it were only the darkest, tiniest chance.

But Laura, who by then had undressed, put on her nightgown and climbed into bed, didn't seem to have any answer for this desperate questioning of the unfairness of fate.

"Calm down, don't get so upset," she said after an interminable silence. And then, sounding like someone trying hard to take stock: "Maybe it's not so bad. Maybe we can go on a trip. There must be countries where all the... all of them live together. (She didn't have the courage to say "dwarves.") We could go there. We could wear silver high-heels, green hats with those pink Amazon feathers that fall to the shoulder, tight dresses with sequins. We could go to the theater every night, with marabou fans and masks. We could go dancing in golden halls filled with streamers, balloons, and Japanese lanterns... read novels with crimes, kidnappings, lots of crimes, lots of kidnappings.... " Her voice was dying away. "Smoke, drink rum, sack the enemy." She was mixing everything up. She was talking about the life of pirates like when she wanted to be a pirate. "Buried treasures, maps, on the island, the parrot...." Here came Robinson. "Friday. Friday, Saturday, Ssssss...." She was asleep. On that "s" that requested and ordered silence, which showed that dwarves also drift off clutching a dream tightly in one hand, like a stone they can throw at the face of anyone who tries to wake them, she drifted off.

I went back to retracing all the days I could remember, back to the first image, the one that slipped from my hands like a fish among the moving sands and blurry waters that had settled at the bottom of my memory. Then, starting from that point, I moved forward. And then back again, and forward once again. Forty, sixty times.

I didn't care whether I had arrived from Paris in a sky-blue cabbage, in a white basket, or in an egg that was almost an Easter egg. The crucial thing was having no parents. Were Felicitas and Chico Dick my parents, or maybe my grandparents, or who?

But the most unbearable part, what made me chew on the edge of the sheet, was my monstrous, pitiful, repugnant condition of being a dwarf condemned to remain a dwarf forever.

Dawn was breaking. I could just make out the sound of the car in the distance. Now I could hear the motor. A horn sounded, far away. It was getting closer. In that celestial carriage, enveloped in that seraphic song, heralded by trumpets played by angels, my mother was coming home.

I kneeled beside the bed and prayed. "May neither the hare nor the partridge cross their path. May the tumbleweeds be scattered by the wind. May those who need to cross the road with their herds sleep a little longer, let them keep sleeping peacefully. Let nothing stop my parents or slow their progress. Let nothing hinder my mother's arrival, may she come right this minute, and may my mother be my mother. Please."

At that moment the bedroom door opened, and María de las Nieves came in. Like a mosaic, her face seemed to be fashioned out of little pieces of guilt, amusement, mockery, of remorse and compassion, but also of fear.

GKY 4

. . .

The leader of the Best Spy Organization in the World and its Surroundings is still sitting in front of the backbone of an unidentified animal (he couldn't find a skull), a lighted candle, and the map where the forbidden zones, the hiding places for messages and the meeting places are all marked with little crosses. Although his face is inscrutable, covered by a mask, I know that X10 the Invincible is Luis María, who is sixteen and the older brother of Miguel and Mariana, and that all kinds of lies pass through the space between his teeth. But as long as he doesn't take off the mask, it can hide every one of the unimaginable faces, or none of them, which would be worse, and even if he does take it off, the face we'd see isn't one of the best—it's a long and petty face, a face like the silhouette of the moon or like a tear or a candle. Maybe that's unfair: his father's is exactly the same, but with intense, watery eyes; his mother's is exactly the same, though always astonished from glimpsing what she shouldn't have seen. Maybe it's all because the three of them play music in church. Miguel's face is different. What I know for sure is that Luis María's face disappears as soon as you stop looking at it, as if a merciful breeze in your memory blew over that low, cold fire that seems to consume it. Anyway, I'd rather see Miguel's face. When you're seeing it, it's what it is and nothing else, no matter what it looks like, and I try to stare off in another direction so I don't have to see that thing that it isn't, but which pulls me toward it, and I turn back to figure out which one is existing inside me, which one it can be when it's not what it is, behind the red mask. Because deep down I always bet on the worst, on what scares me most, on what can hurl me down to the very bottom of the cliff.

But now I'm exhausted, tired even of being afraid. The initiation ceremony has taken too long because there are eight of us: Luis María, Ruth, Miguel, Laura, Bruno and Andrés, Mariana and I. Each one of us has been a winner in the test of cunning, endurance, or courage. So here we are: X10 the Invincible, X8 the Giantess, X7 Keyhole, X6 the Vigilant, X5 and 5X Adam and Shadow—and Vice-versa, they say, since they're twins and it's hard to tell them apart—then X4 the Ghost (underneath my spy badge I've written "GKY," which means God Keep You, but nobody knows it), and finally X1 Tears. A higher number means a higher age and rank.

The boys completed their mission last night, outside that meeting room and in the most dangerous places.

There on the table is the iridescent blue flower vase that we've all seen at some point in broad daylight, fastened with a bronze clamp to Mr. Nino Calcavecchia's burial niche. (Father! Wait for Us! says the inscription, as if Mr. Nino hadn't found any other way to get away from them, from his children who were always in a hurry, jumping into a Ford that was already moving, tossing out packages of goods in every direction, packages that sometimes made a cracking noise as they fell because nobody managed to catch them in flight. As if Mr. Nino had put on a pair of even speedier wings and had left as fast as he could, to deliver the bundle of his soul into the right hands. Mr. Nino who must have stopped to wait for them, seated on the threshold of eternity, killing time by taking out a deck of cards comprised of all the cards in the world, and starting to play out, patiently, an infinite game of solitaire.) At any rate, our leader rescued that flower vase during the night. "Rescued," he says, as if he had won it for this universe by seizing it in a heroic struggle from all the inhabitants of darkness. I don't even want to think about it. And slowly, slowly, as if he weren't afraid of getting infected with death, he strokes that unnecessary trophy, the one nobody but he himself asked him for, just to irrefutably demonstrate his position as our leader, the Invincible One.

And there's the dog mask that Miguel put on, getting down on all fours to bark at the Widow Davies and the Justice of the Peace. ("At two a.m. I saw them from the corner. She opens her black shawl a little and shows him her breasts on the balcony, in the moonlight," Luis María said yesterday. "But no—," answers Ruth, "since the day her husband died she hasn't shown her face on the street, and she looks like a nun behind the window." "So? You think nuns don't have breasts? Or that they're only good for nursing babies?" replied Luis María with a voice that sounded like mortal sin. Ruth blushed beneath her powdered skin and Miguel whistled absentmindedly. Then he said, "We'll see," because spying was his mission, and I felt embarrassed, and under my dress there was a quick movement, a fullness and a shrinking back, a wanting and not wanting to grow up.) Over to the side is the stone the Justice threw at him, and in the air there's still a confusing story that got more and more blurry from misunderstanding, smeared by the smoke from Miguel's cigarette. In one short night Miguel has turned smug and sarcastic. "Naked, on all fours, wearing Mama's fur coat and the mask, I circled the tree four times.... And the widow's shriek, and the judge putting on his glasses to see what I was, or maybe to get a better look at her.... And the window slamming shut.... And here's the stone that hit me. I stood up and ran, and the old man came running behind me, trying to explain about how 'wearing all those mourning clothes makes people hot' and about 'somebody who's really sad and who hasn't had company for years,' almost crying and like he was apologizing to me."

On the floor, outside the bag, are the two geese with twisted necks falling every which way. (But it's better that way than with the ax that chops them, like Pepa axing off the hen's head, and it was horrible to see the cut-off head, but even worse to see the headless body that flew up to the kitchen ceiling, followed by the rain of blood that came down, and the furious beating of the wings, the upside-down, spasmodic fan that was like a feather decoy, and there was no pity, no comfort, although that flight may have been its highest, and even if someday each part recovers the other—or each hen the other hen, since it seemed like there were two and it was impossible to tell which was the more important part—in order to be resurrected among the dead.) And at one side floats the frayed cuff of Bruno's pants, and above that, Andrés's wounded hand, proof of their mad dash around the Larrain estate, with the geese (still alive) honking under their arms. One of them, the one in front, pecking at Andrés's hand; the other, bringing up the rear, looking hopefully toward the dogs that ran nipping at Bruno's heels, the dogs' breath spurring on those speedy fire-heels. Now the boys' heads, bent like the heads of the geese, are held up by a thread of hypocritical modesty. The twin brothers look like they're made of bread dough, their chests swollen with an overdose of yeast. Maybe the two bullets that proclaimed the boys' feat to all the winds of night had been destined to prevent that swelling of chests which now nothing and no one can stop. They're going to float out the window like two expanding lumps of white and spongy dough over the surface of the afternoon, until they deflate and fall, pecked by the detached heads of every unjustly murdered bird.

But the most ignoble spoils of all are those wages, that pile of aluminum tokens that Luis María shuffles in his doubly treacherous hands. It's the price Gaston had to pay for his failure. He refused to set fire to the two stacks of grain in the Otamendis' field, and was immediately kicked out. But just so he wouldn't be considered an enemy from then on, a "spy of spies," he had to turn over all the tokens of the "bestiary" at the theater. (Gaston's mother is in charge of the vestiary, the costume room of the theater, which I've only seen from a distance and which has become, in Gaston's mix of French and Spanish, the "bestiary," that bastion where men and ladies unmask themselves, that stronghold of shamelessness in the form of a counter where they exchange and negotiate their appearances and their skin. That's how, when confronted with a number of smiling horses, I had believed I was face to face with Mr. Ramón Garay, who must have recovered his true skin in the "bestiary;" or on the other hand, following the sinuous movements of Eleonora Guido—that way of sneaking around like a crouched animal that makes her seem to flee elastically from all the betrayed wives and show up on furtive dates with all the deceitful husbands—I've suspected that years ago she stored her skin of a clubbed leopard in there. I pray they'll forget to store it in mothballs.)

I pray to God that all these trophies of masculine courage, all these insignias of crime achieved by desecration, violence, fraud, deceit, and violation in this first pact with man will not be held against any of us. May God deign to accept my portion of payment and expiation.

Because now it's our turn. The boys have freed us from heroic evils and glories, but they condemn us to blindness, to guesswork, to groping for knowledge.

Ruth's test consists of identifying each of us with her hands, blindfolded. I think it's too easy. Miguel has chewed his nails down so far they seem incrusted, ready to disappear into the swollen rim that surrounds them and that flattens out to fit itself gradually all along those thin, anxious fingers. (When he fans them out, it looks as if ten little unhooded ghosts are ready to detach themselves and fly off his hands to go and alight somewhere else.) Laura's hands are hard, firm and smooth-skinned, and since she can flex her fingers at the top knuckles, she shows them facing off, pretending a silly and ceremonious secret meeting of deaf-mutes or a stiff argument between ambassadors from warring parties. Bruno's and Andrés's hands are exactly alike, white, puffy and inexpressive like blind organisms; you could say they're incapable of recognizing or displaying anything, and that they're only good for being hurt at some point, for no particular reason, painlessly, just to show they're hands (but Andrés does have incredibly long nails on his little fingers, which I think he uses to make the holes in the Swiss cheese in their uncle Nicanor's shop). One of Mariana's tiny hands always holds a piece of candy that she drops if she opens her fingers, so the hands that she holds palm-up, cupped in the hope of another piece of candy, are always touchingly sticky and damp with tears. Mine seem bony and astonishing to everybody else, and my uneven and twisted fingers have bird bones, bones I don't know how to keep still, and that's why I sleep with my fists closed tight so they don't let my dreams fall out, so they don't walk away of their own accord. Luis María is the only one left, and it would be pointless to decipher his, because he's the last. And yet, as if it wasn't obvious, just as Ruth's hands paused idly over Miguel's, now Luis María's large flat hands linger over hers, those short fingers oddly curved toward the inside so the hands seem to search for each other—the fingers on the left bent toward the right, the ones on the right bent toward the left—

as if to find themselves around something that I hope isn't anybody's throat. For some time now those hands have been squeezing, lacing, wringing, moving across the surface of Ruth's beautiful hands—so beautiful they are simply beautiful hands—so nobody knows any longer who was supposed to recognize whom, even though nobody even needs to recognize anybody anymore. How long can this go on?

It's Laura's turn. She's already inside the wardrobe. Now come the noises. Laura has to guess who it is and what each of us is doing, and we're supposed to take turns acting out a scene that goes with our new names. Ruth puts a chair on a table and gets up on it and bangs on the ceiling with her fists. "The Giantess touches the sky," says Laura from her upright tomb. "Good!" we all cry excitedly, all except Luis María, who sits still and starts to brandish two knives. Suddenly he takes one and stabs a cushion with a shout, then stifles a cry with his strangler's hand. He starts over, repeating the whole operation three or four times, stops, then stamps the floor with both feet. "The Invincible has vanquished the enemy," says a slightly trembling voice that emerges from the interior of all things. "Close enough," says the other, haughtily self-satisfied, relieving the suspense we all feel. He signals for me to begin. I drag a piece of chain across a single plank, bang it, make it ring against the floor, then I howl like a ghost while I throw a handful of corn against the mirror. I wait. Nothing. I start over. No response. (Do I have to be the one to defeat her? Let her say anything—I'm willing to change what I intended for anything that occurs to her, anything at all, just let her say something.) I repeat my scene. "The Ghost feeds the chickens..." Laura's voice floats out to me, subdued, frightened, and wrong. What I really had imagined was the ghost moving across a cornice in a hailstorm. "Very good!" I shout and clap my hands, while our leader looks at me suspiciously. Now Miguel stands up. He walks toward the wardrobe and knocks three times with his knuckles. He pauses, repeats the act. He does it again, then another pause. Three more knocks, then he bends down and peeks through the keyhole. Had it occurred to Laura to spy out as well? An interminable silence. Then all of a sudden a triumphant voice shouts: "Keyhole looks through the keyhole!" "Bravo!" answers Miguel, banging the door with his palm. Luis María gives him a look of reprimand, reproaching him for that generous gesture. Andrés and Bruno stand up at the same time. "Eva," says Andrés in a lilting tone. "Ave" murmurs Bruno in the same tone. "Adam and Shadow" answers Laura quietly, clearly with the last of her breath. Mariana has been exempted from the test, since she'd only start crying. The door opens like a shining stone being pulled back. Laura comes out of the wardrobe looking pale, but with the expression of someone resurrected into earthly glory. Her hands look like they're shaking.

And what am I doing now inside this sack, with only Luis María nearby, watching to make sure I keep still, and with Mariana who just came into the room and who's supposed to find me, while the others have gone off somewhere so they don't give me away with a glance in the direction of this upside-down well where I am? Better not to think that I've been suspended once and for all over an abyss, between the enemy with its thousand feet and millions of antennae, and my angel of salvation who's turned into an ignorant larva. Better not to think what occupied this sack before me, what rubble of dead, mutilated or disinterred things could suddenly rub against me with unsuspected intentions. What can I think about until Mariana finds me? In the garden, there's the fountain full of little colored fish that seem to dive for those pale gold coins, the treasure that the crucible of light between the branches tosses into the bottom. But inside here the darkness has the color of enclosure, and enclosure has the odor of darkness, surely from now to forever. It's a smell that feels sudden over and over again, as if you were about to be released from it, but then it renews itself and stretches out like those overlong goodbyes, like slow deaths that crush the will of the one who's leaving and the one who stays. It's the smell of a damp glove for perpetual farewells. The darkness has eyes, too, eyes that could be a way out if they didn't multiply until they paralyzed you in your enclosure. Quick, I have to turn them into something else, into a peacock feather, for instance, with gold, black, and green eyelids. When will Mariana get here? I have to avoid the series, because in the darkness each little thing falls with a seed of a thousand similar things, bringing other seeds with them in turn, and they all proliferate when the innumerable gaze of the blackness gazes at them. In the garden is the fountain. I'm going to close each eye of the series with a pale gold coin. No, not the hands either.

Don't let the hands come—not even my own—unless I can know who's behind them. Don't let them start to do things without knowing what they're doing. Grandmother, dear Grandma, where are you coming from? How can you be in bed with your hat on, the three-cornered satin one you wear to church, and why are you stroking my head with a chicken foot? But don't go. No matter what, it's better to have you here covering all the hands and eyes, even with that horrible image. But you do go away, quickly, in your roller-bed, receding to a tiny little luminous point, irretrievable and lost in the formlessness that comes up to devour me. Because Mariana won't ever get here. And it will devour me every night from now on. All my efforts to stay awake, trying to attract the incomprehensible distraction of whiteness, will be in vain. The shapeless thing will come in the very moment I doze off and I'll feel like Jonah in the belly of the whale: a dark organism inside another organism that only throbs and bewilders and filters through its nameless entrails all my faith and my hope, and all my reasons, until it achieves this vacuum in which I float, the absurd pointlessness of everything I try to latch onto, this indefinite suspension of time in which I tenaciously remain. I'm suspended in this hollow mold of existence, and I don't even feel destined to die. But I can't leave, because before leaving this shell I'd have to leave my own organism in which I am imbedded, which they've sewn me into so I'm inside a sack with seams I can't find, with stitches that have no underside, to move me through nothingness toward nothing. Then suddenly I'm no longer suspended and I start to fall, fall in a two-dimensional plane, which is all that's left now in this space inside a foreign organism that doesn't even hold me anymore and through which I tumble inside of myself, completely stripped of any reality, of any cohesion: a handful of particles carried at random toward an unforeseen fate where all that remains is the taste of entrails endlessly devouring themselves, the repugnance felt at their insipid survival or at their still too-vital presence within this void. I am an appendage on this void in which there remains no trace of will or hope, but only a scrap of insistent and senseless memory, while I keep on falling: "At the end there is a garden. At the end there is a garden. At the end there is a garden." Could this be what I came to explore?

And suddenly, unbelievably, there is light, and at the edge of the light Luis María's hands and Mariana's face laughing, laughing uncontrollably for the very first time.

Mission Accomplished

. . .

"Escaping from the hospital," Laura had said, in that way she had of designating each part of the world as if it were a painting, all the while looking us over, satisfied with her work, in our newly inaugurated spy outfits. "Measles and toothache." Precisely. My face is covered with red spots painted on with rouge, and Mariana is wearing a piece of cloth that immobilizes her jaw and opens into a large bow on top of her head. From that moment on, for the past three hours, Mariana and I have been a kind of pitiful, perpetual, painting-in-motion. The scene that is us has crossed the empty streets of town, fleeing from onlookers with a feeling of impossible flight, of spoiled solitude, of endless and irrevocable shamelessness that people in paintings must feel—the ones condemned (no matter what their attitude or appearance may be) to a mercilessly embarrassing exhibition. The odd thing is that from this endless movement we should be spying, though we don't know how, or on whom, or even why—and we're the ones running away, hiding (as if someone were spying on us), when we should be on the lookout for anything strange, anything alive and still able to regret, alter its appearance, or disappear without leaving a trace—all of this until five in the afternoon, which is when we're supposed to report to the Pirate's Tower, next to the Solitary Pyramid.

And if we find something that doesn't change, something invariably suspicious that belongs in turn to another painting, who's to say we won't become a part of that painting, or even get trapped in it? Although I can feel Mariana's sticky hand in mine, and I see her tears and know that if she's not sobbing aloud it's only because she can't open her jaws, I have the feeling we've left behind us, defenseless, our own familiar painting, the painting of our town, the painting of the world, and that we've stumbled into a sinister trap that leads us into a scene I don't know how we'll get out of. I pull up my socks, just to feel a bit safer.

Now we're skirting the edge of the sunflower field. The sun burns over our heads, dazzling us with all that light recondensing at the top of each stem. Every single flower could light up the darkness. But yellow is dangerous. It's an unsettling warning. It's true that when a disturbing sign appears, something has already started to happen: it's more a symptom than a warning of trouble. Spin, sunflower, spin. Yellow spins. Up and down, like riding a tide. I'm dizzy, the dazzling yellow makes me dizzy. I too go up and down, then up, propelled by the void of my stomach, lifted as if on a swing by the beating of my heart. I've begun to be somewhere else, and this isn't happening now. (I'm not going up and down. Someone else is moving me up and down, because I know I'm not running on my own feet. I'm looking back across all the yellow. I'm on the arm of someone who's carrying me, my own arms clinging tight to that someone's trembling neck. I feel that person slipping away, slipping me away, with great, quick jerks. Now I see the red spot. It's blurry. It appears, disappears, and looms up again, always the same distance away. Is it a balloon? A moon wearing war paint? A circle of blood? The blotch comes close, suddenly closer and closer. If it touches us, we'll surely be infected with that mortal, incurable, contagious red. They lower me to the ground. I'm breathing with my eyes closed, a throb of dry green brushing against my face. We make our way between the green that runs crunching and the smell of the dust. Are we going forward or going down? I can't see the red now. It's all a swift whirlwind dragging us toward the taut and pointy barrier that's coming closer. I close my eyes. They reach down and hoist me over, dropping me with a sound of ripping cloth. I fall and roll until someone stops me, gathers me up and presses my head against her chest. It's the same someone who was carrying me. She has a drum inside and she smells like sleep, like gardenias, like letting yourself sink into the bed sheets, like María de las Nieves. I open my eyes and there's the red again, but this time it's in two long bands that run from the shoulder to the hand, separating the edges of a torn sleeve. Nothing else. What was all that? A dream? A memory? Where may I have been looking and where will I find all that's missing?) I open my eyes again, here and now. No sign of Mariana. To one side, the empty street stretches in both directions toward the horizon, where the gray brush lies enveloped in clouds of dust. I call her name three times and wait. I count to three. I call three times again and wait. From across the sunflower field a train's whistle replies, with its hand of dense smoke that passes a lazy finger across the wall of the sky. In my pocket I can feel my spy badge, like an amulet: X4 the Ghost. No, my other name: GKY 4—God Keep You—God keep me and also X1 Tears. Other names would have been better. I call again. Meanwhile, I remember that XI can't talk: her jaws are held together with a gag. How long had I had my eyes closed, sunk into whatever that was? And what if XI Tears tried to call for me and couldn't? It's the hour of La Solapa, the time when the evil lady of the sun roams freely. Maybe she's already appeared in her iguana-shape, with her huge yellow sailcloth hat just like Miss Parrot's hat. Could Miss Parrot be La Solapa? Could Miss Parrot have come in her iguana-shape to carry us off to the depths of her den? Miss Parrot is shut in all day long (or maybe not?—maybe that's when she comes out to look for children who slipped out at siesta time) and she must not like spies very much. Her son Parakeet, with his red beret pulled down over his eyes, walks around with a stick near the entrance to the cave, chasing off anyone who comes near. Red beret? Red beret... and running with a stick? And what if that's what that thing was? Suddenly a bolt of lightning joins all these puzzle pieces that were cut out at different times. I know that I know something, but I'm not sure what. I repeat: La Solapa is the sun lady. She's got the shape of an iguana and she wears an enormous yellow hat and she comes out at siesta time. Miss Parrot has an enormous yellow hat, I've never seen her at siesta time, and she always cries when she talks. Mariana's new name is Tears. La Solapa drags children into her den. Miss Parrot lives in a cave and hates spies. Parakeet has a red cap and chases people away with a stick if they try to come near. A red beret, or a red blotch—I don't know anymore—chased us once, maybe, through these same sunflowers. Chased María de las Nieves and me in her arms, running with her. No. Something's still missing. Where can I look for it? Maybe Mariana, who doesn't know, is figuring it all out right now.

I feel or foresee something stirring among the sunflowers. I climb over the barbed wire fence and realize somehow that I'm moving back into that tremulous and oppressive danger. I move forward with my arms stretched out, pushing aside the sunflower stems. The sound of my own steps follows me as the leaves brush me from behind. I feel like running. But if I run, it will chase me even faster. Nothing like being a spy so you can be spied upon, so everything you set out to scare is crouching there, waiting to scare you. I call Mariana one more time. I have to prove that my voice is really mine, that even if the enemy has taken over my footsteps, he hasn't gotten all of me yet. And then somebody answers. First a low, hoarse moan, then a sound stretching out sharply: the moan of a wounded animal. I make my way in that direction. The sobbing is constant, and it sounds like a muffled rattle. Then the low sound "Lí—" comes to me, as if from inside an iron bell; "—aaaaahhh" comes out of a row of little crystal bells cracked by sadness. I call to her not to move, I'm coming. My voice rushes out too strong, then stops, because there's Mariana, her gag fallen down around her neck like a poorly tucked napkin, and she's looking at me with all the terror in the world, as if someone had fed her some monstrous food, a bite of the worst nightmare: a sweet roll made of tar or a cockroach compote.

Behind Mariana I can see the spot, the huge blotch. It's a blackish red, damp and sticky. On top of it, the head of a man who doesn't move. It looks like he's gone to sleep face-down, his shapeless gray hat fallen over his neck and his stiff arms at his sides. He's wearing a ragged shirt that's dirty white, dirty ochre, or dirty gray, and blue pants stained with lime and oil, completely frayed, ending almost in fringes at the ankles. Yellow shoes gleam surprisingly on his feet, so new they look like he just stepped into them. It's as if he tried them on for the first time when he was already asleep. I stare at it all, and a cloud of smoke and emptiness invades me.

Mariana's arms circle my waist and she's crying against my shoulder, crying, crying relentlessly, repeating untiringly a phrase I can't make out, while I, entranced, see this as the trap through which we entered into the frozen scene of that other painting. We've got to escape before it locks us in, before we're paralyzed. We have to move our scene to the other side of the picture without taking this one with us, without staying stuck inside it. Finally I can make out her words: "Lía, Lía, the man with the sack." Then I see the sack, fallen to one side, filled to the brim with the body of mystery, swollen with the whole volume of the unimaginable. I have to decide. If we go forward, after a few steps we'll come out by the tracks; if we go backwards, we'll only repeat the long road of the chase and the escape. The first option is a complete unknown: the length of the rope that ties me to home and safety runs out long before that, and the rope might be cut completely. The second option is familiar: I was victorious already, though who knows over whom, or when, or how, and besides, this way is protected by the laws of obedience.

I make up my mind. I lift Mariana up and she wraps her arms around my neck. I take two or three steps back, hearing the rustling of the yellow jungle behind me. The man hasn't moved. I spin around and start to run, with a waterfall of tears on my back. It isn't easy. Mariana weighs too much and I have to work hard to both hang onto her and push the sunflower stems out of the way at the same time. I don't dare look back to see if the blotch is chasing us. When I feel the stickiness or the hand, I'll know, but then it will be too late. We'll fall right into the sack. Even so, it's almost impossible to run. It's like a dream. The density of the air is different; it's turned into a density for feathers, just when you weigh more than ever before, and the leg stretches out to take a step or to jump as far as possible, but instead the foot falls back by its mate, an unknown quantity, all its strength gone. It's worse than in a painting. It's running inside an eye made of soft glass where the air can't get in to erase the stare. We've got to get out somehow before the glass hardens and fuses us, before we're trapped forever inside the gaze that holds the spot and the man. I don't even want to think about the sack. Without stopping, I shift the weight of the sobbing. Is Mariana looking now at that red I was looking at... when was that? Four years from now, will she also wonder with what feet she fled, who-knows-when and from who-knows-what? I hope she'll wonder and I'll be able to tell her, if she's been lucky enough to forget. I hope we can get out of the eye and the spot without falling into the sack. "Our Father who art in heaven"—if I get to twenty, I win. There it is, the place where the taut and prickly barrier rises up. It's the barbed wire fence. Without stopping, I gather Mariana up and lift her as high as I can, letting her drop to the other side. I jump—the way María de las Nieves must have jumped years ago—and fall. I take Mariana by the hand and we keep running. We must have the blotch stuck to our backs.

The street is empty. The sun is still piling dust clouds on the horizon. But at last everything that protects me comes into sight: the chinaberry tree across from the Albarellos' house; the gray-faced stranger with dull hair and dead eyes, with her velvet heart pierced by a thousand pins, propped in the doorway of the Casa Millán; the black hen that tries to fly when we pass, and keeps flapping her wings, flapping forever at the same height without ever descending (like Nanni's aria); and further on, our corner and the garden gate. It doesn't matter if they see us: "Measles and Toothache." It's better if they see us. Chinaberry, mannequin, hen: they will be our witnesses in this frantic race that cannot last. Wood, wax, feathers, they will cry with whatever voice God might give them so they can stop the abduction and denounce the culprit. "Objection! Objection! Objection!" cries the hen, raising the alarm. But she's so stupid she wouldn't know how to explain a thing. Bad luck to count on her as an ally, the only witness for our defense. But thank you anyway, thanks all the same. I only hope you don't end up at the bottom of the sack as well.

Three more steps. There. Mission accomplished.

I give the gate a push and we go into the yard. Laura is sitting on a marble bench.

X6 the Vigilant, with an open black eye painted over each lid, is sleeping, oblivious to everything, not spying in our direction, not even looking toward this side of the painting.

And Then They Were Gone

. . .

Maybe these two stair-stepped walls connected at the top really are the ruins of the Pirate Tower, as Miguel claims. Once I heard someone say there used to be an ocean here. Now there's nothing but sand. Sometimes when we're going down the road in the carriage, you can see the water receding and we never reach the place where it is. It's like an awful game, the dead water transformed into a ghost: it's the poisonous blotch, only backwards, the blotch that is pursued but you can never touch it. It makes you feel a sense of urgency about getting there, a thirst, but then it's a lie. If it weren't a lie, the carriage would have to move under water on certain days, and maybe right now if I look at my house from here, I'll think it's drowning. Or maybe these two walls that come together to charge the dunes, one edge already crumbled away, are really part of a sunken ship as Laura says, and then all the rest is true, except for the Pirate Tower, and probably a whole lot more. But inside there are lofts with smaller boats in bottles among the smoke-colored spider webs, and even aquariums misted over by the breath of dying mother-of-pearl, and dolls with jointed limbs resting like blue herons on the stairs that are no longer coming or going anywhere and are fixed in every direction like the spokes of a wheel—all of it embalmed, nothing visible through an air bubble where the sand begins to rush in suddenly, as through a keyhole, so that no one from the inside can look out at this sloping dune, which in that case would be the sky where I'm tracing these little lightning bolts with a stick. Or maybe these two joined walls with a triangular opening at the top are really the ruins of a castle facing the sea, which is what I believe, and then all the rest is true, and maybe much more if you switch the places of the ship and the tower. And someday I'll go up again to that window carrying a lamp of live fireflies, waiting for the ship to really and truly return, across water and not sand, slowly, almost motionless as it passes between the castle and the tower, its sails like an angel's robes puffed out by the wind, and then everything will begin again in a miraculous story that I don't yet know, but that will be told by everything I find, everything that will have to be deciphered in order to start telling it again from where it was interrupted when the sand came.

If I got up on the three stacked crates right now and looked out through the triangular opening, I'd see only the dune that tilts up from the road almost to the opening, the same dune you can see from below if you go around to either side of the walls. If I went around either of the walls and looked in from outside, without using the crates, I'd see what I see now: the Solitary Pyramid, that enigmatic column broken off at six feet without reaching anything—at least anything visible. And seated around its base, Luis María facing this way and all the rest of them with their backs to me. From left to right, Ruth, Miguel, Laura, Bruno, Andrés and Mariana. From right to left, X1 Tears, X5 and 5X Adam and Shadow, X6 the Vigilant, X7 Keyhole and X8 the Giantess.

X4 is missing. Missing and not missing, because it's me: X4 the Ghost. But for Luis María I'm not missing. Why doesn't he go ahead and start? It's not me he's waiting for, since he sees me. He also sees that I see him, though maybe he doesn't know that I would rather not see him, unless he had never put those shoes on. I have to do something while I kill time. I could tell myself a story while I sit between the two walls that come together, but even the story of the two connecting walls is always tied to that same thing, no matter how I try to not see it or refuse to even name it. "I'm walking down a little road..."—and the sunflowers start to grow and the dead man appears, face down on the red blotch. "I'm hiding under the bed," and the sunflowers start to grow and the dead man appears. "Someone is knocking at the door," and the sunflowers start growing. "I'm not me," and that's it. I was wrong. I should have told someone when I got home with Mariana, after we'd seen him. But no one was there, just Laura the Vigilant asleep on a garden bench with two wide-awake eyes painted over her closed eyelids, and when we came back out she wasn't there anymore. After that I couldn't get rid of the dead man. I washed my face three times, I rinsed out my mouth because it tasted like trembling and like everything that has to do with shaking: dirt, blood, and sackcloth; I closed and opened my eyes several times, pushing him out; I thought light and white everywhere, so he wouldn't be there. But it didn't work, he settled in. On our way back I told Mariana that the man was a product of our disobedience and the siesta, and then he wasn't there anymore; that inside a drawer I had no reason to open, I had once found an onion with very long fingernails that never stopped growing, and that once when I tried to go into a room that I had no reason to go into, the space of the door was suddenly covered by a loose hand that all at once turned into a spider with transparent bones, and then they were gone. Only then did Mariana stop crying, although everything had gotten worse. Yes, I should have told someone, but I couldn't. And by the time we got here, Luis María's shoes were already here.

Now he's doing roll call. Every head (except Ruth's) is turned toward me, chin down and shaking, while they hold their hands up and wave them rhythmically. Shoulders lifting and falling. Heads and backs again.

I have my reasons for not going in. I still don't know what I'm going to do, and if I went in I would probably tell it all, all at once, since I know that if I say it I'll share it with each of them. But there's someone among them who has gone his own way, and that's exactly what keeps me from going. Besides, it's foolish to think what I'm thinking. Do I believe I'm going to get rid of the dead man just by telling? I'm the one who saw him. How am I going to stop seeing him, even if the rest of them imagine him until they see him too? Would I be able to keep just the bloodstain, or the head with no face, or the sack? And who's to say that one part all by itself wouldn't become something even worse—that it wouldn't grow all out of proportion? Especially the sack, since I don't even know what's inside. All right, I won't start daring it to open now. But I'm not going in, either, until it's my turn. It's better staying here, sitting where the sand hollows itself out like a nest to incubate stormy weather. The storm must be a gray beast, something between a dog and a wolf, with worn teeth and moth-eaten skin. When it's born, someone will name it Lulu, or Fox, or Jasmine, or any other silly thing so they can prove they're its master, and they won't even know what they have in their house.

Now the heads turn toward Ruth. Some bend forward to get a better look. A better look at what? It's just like in the theater or at the races. Except that it's just Ruth, no chance of anything else. What can Ruth be telling them she saw? A horse grazing behind a wire fence, a shop window full of jars of white ointment, a woman foolishly brushing her hair in front of a mirror. Yes, that's it. That's why she's undoing the mop of hair tied at her neck, letting it fall over her shoulders and back, shaking her head, brushing Miguel's face with it, wrapping him in clouds of yellow mane, acting like a captive coming home fifteen years after the Indian raid. And what's so strange about a woman combing her hair, unless the hair suddenly bursts into flame, or maybe a couple of doves fly out? And if the woman had taken off a wig, what would Ruth be doing now? It's not just my impression: Miguel bends his head between his arms to yawn, and the others are starting to think vaguely about other things.

As for Luis María, I'd rather not watch the way he taps his feet impatiently, as if he weren't taking those shoes into account.

No. Even if you whistle or call for me, I won't go. You should know better than anybody, Luis María. Or else you'll suspect it when you see my face, as soon as you know for sure about my terrified, obligatory to and fro, heel and toe, toe and heel, even though I didn't want to. It'll be much worse for you than for the rest, except for me, since the dead man doesn't care about anything but maybe pursuing me from the inside. He's not even going to be there when God calls him, if he keeps chasing me in this first judgment. Of course, the last judgment will be different: He raises a finger, without even naming anyone, and a long path opens and you make your appearance. It won't be a matter of not answering or trying to hide. Maybe you don't even have to tell anything: He knows it all. But He won't spare us that shame in the presence of the others, those down below, on the heap, in the wheel. If He called me now, maybe I wouldn't even have to say: "My pity was a weakness, it was a weapon of torture that wounds both sides; my integrity was pride; my charity, a mirror of shame; my humility, a little crease in my ambition to become you—and I'm still not sure I am not you; my faith, a form of hunger, and the kiss I give the leper is a measure of heaven that doesn't lessen my disgust and that doubles his suffering." Please go away, Mr. Dead Man. Don't increase your sins with me—and take your sack with you too. Maybe inside there's something that can serve as evidence or extenuating circumstance. Or maybe there's another dead man just like you, in a puddle of blood next to another sack that holds another dead man. And why not the same succession from inside out? We would all be with you inside a sack, and the dead man outside would be another, and we would all be repeated outside as well, and then there would be another sack and another dead man outside of it, all the way to God, who encloses us all and who can be the final you, since He's the only one who knows the contents of the successive sacks, inside out or outside in. And what if the very first sack held nothing but another pair of shoes?

I tell you I'm not going in yet, Luis María. When I reached the end of that other path, I would be your denunciation, even if I said nothing. For the moment, let's stay away from the complicity or the accusation that would tie me forever to your shoes.

Once again, the faces turning around and the flapping of the hands. The shoulders moving up and down. Heads and backs, again. And then Laura's clean profile, and Ruth's, powdered like a moth, turning toward Miguel like two medallions flanking Saint George or Prince Valiant. I can't imagine what Miguel saw. In everything he tells there are always people on all fours, armies of people looking for a button, or children who are born shouting "Land!" or trains heading right through a room and you've got to set the alarm clock to let them pass, or scenes in which four hundred and thirty nine spies carry the same badge on their lapel, usually an eye that lights up like a lantern and burns out like an eclipse, and all his stories end victoriously with the spirited pirate song that says "I am the terror of the land!" or with some mysterious phrase like "All this happened while the main character was still alive." The truth is that for Miguel, the night is more nocturnal, disguises are more disguised, distances are shorter. Suddenly the voices get louder and there is applause. Luis María shakes his head, argues, restores order by raising his arms like a conductor. Ruth pokes Miguel's arm with her elbow, as if I couldn't see her. Bruno glances my way like a red bubble about to burst, and Andrés looks like he's got a bone stuck in his throat. I'd bet that Laura is winking at me, because even from here I can tell the difference between the painted and the open eye.

It's over. Miguel is coming toward me with a triumphant air, mocking and indifferent, which makes my cheeks hotter the closer he gets. Will the stain be visible on me? I'm tied to the dead man and to Luis María by that viscous, indestructible, persistent spreading thing that prevails over all other colors, over all the avidity of the sand. I'm alone with them, sunk into the same substance, the same guilt that must be terrible, much more contagious than any illness. In contrast, that tanned skin, that lock of straight hair, the face that sums up all the faces of the future, all these are innocent; that white shirt with rolled-up sleeves, those knee-length pirate pants, all infused with Miguel's unbearable glow, are free of any stain; those bare feet that come to rest, lacking the nostalgia or the regret over shoes, cannot be witnesses or accomplices, cannot be guilty of anything.

If I look up he'll see me crying. And when I hear his words, I wish I had the head of an egg, or a pin, or a blind worm: "Princess, this is no castle, nor is it a ship. It is the Pirate Tower, as thou well knowest. They await thee at the base of the Solitary Pyramid, so thou canst give account of thy mission. But thou art not a prisoner here; thou canst grow old, sneeze, or turn into a dove. And if thou shouldst wish to flee, thou mayst count on my sky-blue horse, my cape, my sword, and my flag."

By now I feel I don't have any head at all, only dislocated fragments of some fragile material that has been subjected to all the temperatures of shame and stress, and that's when he leans over and says, unceremoniously:

"If you don't want to go, don't go, or don't say anything; either way, our leader is a traitor."

"LíaLíaLíaLíaLíaLíaaaaa!" The voice becomes many voices, raised and intermingled, coming from the base of the pyramid.

The bare feet move off toward the left in a sandy cloud. Now I look at him. It's no longer Miguel, but the tower sentinel who goes up the broken stairway, which is one of the walls, cupping his hands to his mouth and shouting "Lía"—ahead, toward the place where he knows I'm not, covering all the other cries with that name that goes rolling over the dunes. "Líaaaa!" will be from now on another mirage, different from that of the sea, a similar nostalgia but one belonging to me, above the other voices that will call for me where I am not, in some place where I cannot answer back. I can still see him illuminated against the sky, hand cupped over his eyes—according to him, high in the tower, according to me, high in the castle—, launched resolutely into another adventure, into another character, into another fantasy that doesn't match mine.

Yes, our leader is a traitor. I can point to one of the signs. That doesn't free me from the guilt of having seen; in fact, it will probably increase my guilt, even double it. Three. Three little pieces of coal appear when I stir the sand around with this little stick, as if I were consulting the quarries of destiny. Three pieces of some unfathomable substance, purified by fire, proclamation, and anticipation of the forges of that hell in which I will burn for three separate but unequal sins: being victim, executioner, and judge. Three sins that add up to not being God. What can I do now? It's too late for being born, but too early to have to die. Let's stir the sands once again. Buried luck produces the illusion of choice, even though it's the same luck for everyone until we become God again. And that object rising and rising, isn't it a silvery dove? Isn't it the gleam of a wing that I can't look at with open eyes because it shines too brightly?

"LíaLíaLíaLíaLíaaaa!" It takes flight from the chorus and wings its way up through the air in successive bursts, together with the luminous gliding that I direct upwards and downwards as I please, following it now behind my closed eyelids. If I follow those movements upwards, my eyes will turn inward and backward. Maybe that's where I have to look. What could a wing be searching for in the darkest part of me?

"Lía! Lía!" It's Laura's voice and the weight of her hand on my shoulder. I look. She's standing in front of me with one hand holding the huge straw bonnet from Italy that Aunt Adelaida lets her wear on Mondays from two to five.

"What's the matter? Were you asleep? Weren't you listening? Why aren't you coming?"

"Nothing. No. Yes. I don't want to."

She blinks. The other gaze, the one she painted on her eyelids to feign wakefulness when she's asleep, moves up and down, passing in a dark, dead flash over the living gaze.

"Let's go, come on!"

"I'm coming. When it's my turn. I have to think."

"It's your turn now. Come on—you can think later."

"No. I have to think about what I'm going to say."

"Are you going to lie?" she asks, almost in a whisper, willing to help me. Then, turning her head, "Let's go!"

"I don't know. What did you see?"

"Me? Not a thing, I fell asleep. I made up some story, but they didn't believe me."

"What about the others?"

"Ruth saw a horse grazing behind a wire fence. . . ." (I know, I saw the mane that brushed Miguel's face.) "It was grazing, then it looked at her, and then went back to grazing, then looked at her, and like that. Bruno and Andrés didn't see anything. They hid under the dining room table. When the clock struck three, they almost saw the cuckoo—almost, because when they stuck their heads out, the little door had already closed. The same thing happened at 3:30."

She holds out her hand to me, without letting go of the bonnet, and drags me forward.

"And what did Miguel see?" I ask as I stand and look up, not seeing him. And while we walk and I look for him—because my salvation can only come from one or the other of them—Laura answers as if in a quick prayer:

"Miguel saw the devil going into the maid's room. He said the devil had Luis María's face, but faster feet" (the feet, yes, the feet) "—and he couldn't catch up with him. When Miguel got there, the devil shut the door in his face. He ran around to the window, but the other was already closing the shutters. Through a crack, he caught a glimpse of white clothes fluttering around, and two red faces, burning in hell, and he could have sworn. . . . But he couldn't tell us any more, because Luis María got really angry and shouted, and Miguel went to stand guard in the tower, to keep a look out, and be careful: the devil is watching us and hearing me, too—" And then, speaking to our leader, with the solidity of evidence behind her, "Okay, we're coming. You won't get anywhere questioning her, see for yourself. She saw the same as I did."

I don't believe you're the devil, Luis María, though there is something in that. I'm looking at you for the first time as if you were and were not the devil, while I take a seat beside Mariana. The long nose that falls farther than it should; the mouth like one eating its lips or cauterizing its lies; those close-set eyes, the better to watch each other, with the look of a candle going cold; that flat, angled chin always tediously negotiating more space; the flesh with the color of a worm under a flowerpot suddenly exposed, and all this in a face pulled to the left by a petty and hypocritical tacking thread, all this has to ooze out at those feet. Those feet attract me as if they were following me; they attract me with the appearance of the unbelievable. They seem huge, unusual, sudden. They're like a name I don't know, but that I might learn at any moment: they are the involuntary and blind expression of accusation.

I can't help it. I always go back to the feet, even if I try not to. Even if we so often discover each other from the feet up, I can't manage to retreat to the other side in this battle between hawk and dove. I can't believe the feet aren't uncomfortable, that they don't shrink back as if they felt ants or fear or injustice, and not because I'm accusing, but only because they are who they are and I am here, which means the same. Maybe any exterior time is swifter than my interminable dove-time. Maybe not even ten seconds pass before his eyes get round and the heavy hawk-lid makes an effort not to fall, to hold itself up in the air. It stays up. I see it when his pupils contract and Luis María says:

"What did you see?"

And I feel myself falling with a brief and desperate wing-flutter that shakes me all the way from his face jutting forward to the escape toward those ignorant feet, which if they knew would prefer not to be here, or else to be here until the end, so that tomorrow someone could say, "And then they were gone."

"What did you see?" His voice sounds distrustful, mocking, surprisingly high.

I turn back to his face. It came forward and stopped, sure of its attack. I measure the distance for my retreat: none left. I'm up against a transparent wall. I'm getting pinned between two panes of glass, like a shiny insect or like the little illustrations of the martyrs.

"What did you see?" Does he really want me to tell? If I tell what I saw, he'll know for certain what I am seeing, though he can only have suspected it until now. If I don't add what I'm seeing now, the rest of them won't learn anything, but I will begin to create with him an organization within the organization, a shady association full of allusions, implications and omissions. There will be a sly extortion with the force of his guilt and the weakness of my silence, and I'll be stuck between the panes, doomed to respond to him like his own shadow. If I tell what I saw and what I'm seeing, he'll be able to lie or make up excuses. At least then they'll all know. But I'll torture myself from now on, since my accusation, which could easily seem like his victory, will have surpassed his guilt, which will then crumble into dust over me, into nothing. Not only will I pardon him for any revenge, I'll provide it to him in payment, and this jousting of humiliation and indulgence will go on forever. Both of us will be trapped between the panes, spying on each other. And why do we have to remain locked in this absurd mutual dependence, in this unbearable complicity, until someone else comes to judge us, and even after that—unless after that we'll be gone too?

"Nothing..." I say slowly. I've made up my mind: I'm with the dead man. I won't share him with anyone. I'm taking him with me until he devours me or until I'm not here anymore. "I didn't see anything. Anything at all," I repeat, preferring to stay with his feet as well, his enormous feet that offend and beg pity, rather than with the face that includes them and so much more. "Not a thing."

It's over. I broke the pane behind me. I can keep moving backwards until I fall into total darkness with the dead man.

"The man!" shouts Mariana at that very moment, and she grabs my hand with her little hand that's not sticky from candy because it's gloved in sand.

I hadn't counted on this. All around me I feel a movement of mice being aroused, ready to expel me from the darkness if I don't move alone toward the pane in front.

"The man with the sack..." Mariana insists, crying, rubbing her eyes with the other glove of sand.

"What man?" asks Luis María, lips puckered to whistle, pretending to see in the distance the limits of his patience.

Is this a challenge? I'm ready to stand facing the glass in front.

"She saw the same thing I did—didn't I tell you?" interrupts Laura, just in time.

"The dead man, face down in a puddle of blood."

How could Laura have known? When could she have seen him? She told me she had told them a lie. But Luis María isn't so sure it's a lie, or else he believes that one of Laura's lies plus the same one of mine could add up to a truth, or else he believes, as I do, that Laura saw without looking what I saw by looking, because his tightened mouth is motionless, a bubble opened outward on the surface of the dough, though right away he says:

"Oh, right! Stories, the same old story! The man on the floor, next to the half-opened wardrobe door, and the hand that appears slowly and drops a dagger. Did you dream the same thing as your sister?"

No, it's not the same. I'm missing the wardrobe, the hand, and the dagger. I'm missing the dream and I've got more than I need of some other reality.

"Counterspy sightedddddd!" shouts the guard loudly from the top of the tower.

Everyone is startled. There's an instant of indecision, then a jump and a blur of dust. Turning my head, I just manage to see Miguel's puffed-out shirt and the flash of his diving disappearance below. The dizzy whiteness of a falling curtain passes swiftly over the triangular window. Meanwhile the dust cloud has gone off in a single direction. It flies toward the wall on the right and cuts off the escape of Laura, Bruno, Andrés, and Ruth. Luis María turns around once before he disappears with Mariana held aloft under his arm. It's a mask that sums up resentment, threat, and curse, and I see it only briefly, at the moment in which the guard announces from far off, his voice muffled by the wind, the struggle and the wall:

"Hostage taaaa-ken!"

I stand up slowly and walk over to the three stacked crates. I climb laboriously, amidst the noises of a stormy beach, a surf that deposits an enemy ship among the cliffs, and the smothered shouts signaling the heroism of the tower guard. I'm going up to the high window of the castle, where my fate as heroine begins. It ends exactly at the level of the dune on the other side, at the same height as me. Opposite these walls that come together, not as a tower or a ship, nor as a castle, the voices join around a castaway in white overalls who sinks into the dune under Miguel's weight, and it's Gaston.

"That's enough! Who's the leader here?" thunders Luis María. His previous mask disappears under a different, trembling mask, unbearably misaligned as he says, "And what now? Let's get out of here."

Maybe it just seems to me, maybe it's not true that his words vibrate like a jiggled photograph or an emulsion that's been stirred. Gaston struggles face-up beneath Miguel, his knees between Miguel's, his wrists pinned by the pale hands. He's another trapped insect, not an insect on display between two windows, but an insect in open air. Poor Gaston! He can't even move forward or backward to break the glass, it occurs to me in the exact moment when my own panes may be raising themselves again, since he says:

"That's all I know. He's old and he's dead. They think he jumped from a freight car and made it that far, because the blood starts right beside the tracks. Nobody knows who he is. His socks are torn and he doesn't have any shoes on. I swear, that's all I know. Now let me go!"

Miguel stands up. He lifts Mariana up and hoists her onto his shoulders. Running downhill, galloping sideways toward the road, he lets out a perfect whinny that sounds something like "Let's go seeeeeeeee!"

Bruno and Andrés follow him, tumbling down the sandbank. They look like two cylindrical dolls joined at the feet, two foolish ship's boys made of striped wood: blue, white and blue, white and blue. Laura runs in a zigzag, still holding onto her bonnet, dragging Ruth by the belt, who stumbles forward in the dance of a disjointed puppet. Gaston descends carefully, arms held out, taking quick little sparrow-steps. Keeping his distance, Luis María brings up the rear. One big step and a skate with two bare feet, one big step and a skate: two bare feet marking the confession of the evildoer in the middle of the dunes.

And, from the window in these walls that will never again be a castle, or a ship, or a tower, I look for a moment at the shoes left behind, and I pray that castle, ship, and tower may burn in the conflagration of the late afternoon sun, that they turn to ash and fall over this burning sand that will never be the sea, that the ash may cover the yellow shoes, the stolen shoes, the dead man shoes, so that when I open my eyes they won't be there anymore, so that tomorrow I can say, "And then they were gone."

Why Are Begonias So Red?

. . .

They didn't have to go through the underbrush but going there was part of the dangerous adventure. It had rained and the afternoon light, after filtering into the clearing, was absorbed, without ever reaching the ground, by the fallen leaves: pale greenish disks, ready to fly off in their near transparency; minuscule half moons forged of luminous yellow, sequins of old gold, somber green needles shattered by the sun's force, wings of faded gauze gleamed against the dark humid background. It looked like a surprising sky. For a few moments it made me dizzy, like every sky that looms too close to us. I'd have liked to cut off a swatch and take it with me. (What a sky patched together from scraps of various different cosmogonies that I can assemble with those that formed a backdrop for the eternity of certain days! If I could come to life again in that sky made up of all skies! It won't happen. It fades suddenly, washed away by a single teardrop. It fades with a sound of sand, with a fistful of sand flung wide, revealing a white ceiling that will remain enclosed within my eyes forever when I shut my eyes forever.) There goes the scissor-tailed flycatcher. They should be snipped into bits before they reach here, before they go off; they should leave me only this sky of moist earth cut across by the constellation of "The children who never came back."

Can one walk through this great black cloud? Or will it turn out to be a hole through which we'll fall to another earth? No. Somber tree trunks surround us: sentries of coal, black legions of penitents. This is the part that burned. In the middle of the night, the blazing forest must have looked like an apparition, a delirium in the midst of fever. I don't know whether I saw it. It might be a memory I made up and I can't change it. I come to it abruptly at the end of a hallway, beside my bed, under water. It appears like a hallucinated future Christmas that was promised me for some dark moment. It is beautiful. And nevertheless, it was prepared by the murderer's hand, that hand that failed to be warmed by four bodies destroyed by a flameless fire. I don't want to imagine it; I don't want it to turn into another memory for the future.

The forest ends here. With these eucalyptus trees that undress to the point of tearing off strips of their skin hardened by harsh exposure. The underbrush begins here, the path hazy, barely traced out against the high grass and spiky weeds. He went through here dragging along that hell that burst into flames a few steps farther along. Some hundred and fifty feet farther along is the house, with its corrugated tin roof, red and faded, its ochre walls, and green windows taken over by vines. That's where the crime took place. And why didn't he burn the house down if that was what he wanted to destroy? No, it wasn't that, nor to escape justice; he didn't try to wipe out any traces; he didn't even try to run away. Didn't they find him sitting there calmly under a tree, with his hands in his pockets? It was his own hell, but they didn't give him time. They found him too soon. They may have only managed to prolong his swan song.

I take hold of Laura's hand and I keep walking, almost without breathing so as to not inhale the indestructible edges of the hell and the crime. Laura's other hand is hidden in the huge pocket that stretches from her hem almost up to her waist. No doubt that hand is busy in that absurd gesture of hers that consists of rubbing her thumb between her index finger and her middle finger, a gesture they keep scolding her for, I never understand why. She says it brings her luck. I look at her out of the corner of my eye; her eyes are half closed under her piqué bonnet. Should I do the same thing? Does she half close her eyes in order not to see, or in order to see farther? Is it better to see clearly rather than imagine things into the haze? Miguel whistles, indifferent, with his hands in his pockets, but he isn't fooling me. Is he holding tight to a black stone with green veins, a penknife that can't possibly be useful, or a lucky talisman made of fish bones? If he'd hold my hand I'd dare to breathe deeper, perhaps, if something weren't beginning to jump up and down inside me. I don't want to look at Ruth. I don't like her codfish eyes, blue and absorbed, or her white skin that seems covered in flour (ready for frying, but with scales), or her too-small mouth, tightened in a gesture of whim or disdain, as if she disliked the fish bowl. On the other hand, she's so tall that her gaze never takes me in; she's always looking over my head. I wonder what's happening over my head?

I like the crunch of the grass, although it sounds as though someone's walking along with us, doesn't it? There's no one. But I'd rather walk in the same place, even when it doesn't make any noise, because noise shifts us, pulls us along in the trembling grass with a long shiver and deposits us all in front of the house, facing the porch. Dust, unfinished stories, vestiges of an unreconstuctible era that nevertheless breathes on, lurking in all we see.

What Miguel is doing is useless. You don't have to try the latch to know that the door is closed—and that he isn't defending us from anything. We follow him in silence while he pushes with no result against the two windows blinded by dark shutters; while he heads on decisively, stepping on the empty flowerbeds and moving along the wall, toward the large window on one of the sides, which offers the same resistance; while he moves into the rear gallery, framed by the worm-eaten wooden handrail with its flaking paint; and he stops in front of his hope, which is exactly the beginning of that hell that will continue to live on in me.

There's a broken pane of glass and a dark gap. They both give us the idea that it might be possible to keep pushing the latch back, getting a hand in there, and part of an arm, and managing to turn something on the inside, on the side away from the familiar faces and what those eyes can see before falling, those eyes that still insist upon seeing. The arm returns, the hand pushes. "It's not opening even though it's unlocked!" (It's like asking death not to kill me, like asking to be remembered in forgetting; although this might rather be: "It's not closing even though it's closed!") It won't open, however much Miguel pounds on it with his fists. I'd almost rather that someone answer from an impossible mouth. Then we could run away. Perhaps I should do that in any case but Miguel blocks my way—even if he hadn't moved, he'd block my way just by being there—because he takes three steps back and hurls himself forward with all his strength concentrated in his right shoulder. The window shutter spins out as if it were being ripped off. In the space that opens and includes me, a picture to be seen with one's eyes closed appears and stuns me. A ray of golden dust crosses it diagonally; it flows and forms a bright spot in the lowest part, a sediment of incriminating gold, the blood of butterflies affected by the crime. Why does the haze of time fly downward and condense? No doubt to illuminate the place where it happened. Now some shapes begin to appear, shapes that may only be immobilized by surprise, that may be looking at us. And suddenly Miguel bursts into the interior of the picture. We follow him; I am last, with a wing of frost. The first thing that appears are the pictures within this picture that we've just destroyed and the round face of the grandfather clock. It's missing its hands; it could be any hour and none. It has lost in authority but gained in forewarning. Then the living room looms up, unhurried and unsleeping: the three armchairs of greenish silk with faded roses, the console under the golden frame, the big broken mirror, invaded by the dying reflection of moss and ferns that are not here, that must be in some other room or they've been taken away already, the piano—locked with a key, Miguel has just checked—no doubt soaked with water. Because even though everything smells of dust, it all looks as though it's under water. There's something that drowns me in these faded golds, in these submerged greens, and it's not just that agitated sea I've just discovered on the wall in front of me, although this sort of thing is always happening to me. First I feel it and then what I've been feeling appears, as if I've created it. Not the ship; the ship doesn't have anything to do with it. It tips, though, menaced and menacing, with sails tense under the storm winds that subside and flare. Farther out, in those other framed pools, there, too, the faces of the drowned begin to surge toward the surface. If I look at them, they'll catch me, they'll drag me down to the bottom.

That's why, when Laura opens the living room door and walks through it, I follow her, without asking myself what I'm going into.

We're in the vestibule, facing the door Miguel wasn't able to open, that probably hasn't been opened for entry since it was closed at departure. (How much opening and closing, entering and leaving; I no longer know whether you leave by opening or enter by closing. Is every step a door and that's what time is? A world of windows would be better. "A world of windows that look out onto a door?" the little enemy voice asks in me, ever alert. Enough. I'll close the windows, too.) But that's not how it is. Someone came in afterward from somewhere else, because there are remains of burned wood, papers, ashes, and an empty tin can in the alcove under the stairs. From there we can barely discern, through torn curtains, a dismantled dining room in the dim light. Before we could begin to make out the heads of those eating, we are climbing up the stairs; there's a stairway, and anywhere there's a stairway, Laura and I can't think of anything but climbing it, without a thought as to whether we'll be able to come down again. It's a kind of irresistible upward moving vertigo: the attraction of mystery and the velocity of fear. On my skin I feel the bubbles of icy air as they breathe me up in fits and starts through a funnel that begins in the pit of my stomach. My skin contracts in a sour harshness, like the taste of green pears, or like the shiver of snagged satin. Sometimes I feel it when I'm on a swing, sometimes when Miguel's look or his arm brushes me. But this funnel is black and this satin is black. I go up anyway, on tiptoe behind Laura, who is also tiptoeing. Some of the steps creak a lot, all along their length from one end to the other. The boards of the landings complain the loudest. I feel the harshness even in my teeth. Is it my own taste, the taste of my last moments that speed by through the tube that sucks me up? Finally we emerge into a space of red tiles dimmed by dust; the dust that must also be dimming the blood that stains them. Without the dust, we'd be sure to see it in the light that comes in the skylight. "Huge puddles of blood" they always say. And of course, "Why here?" No, it wasn't here. "The model father, a good son and a better husband, who killed four innocent people in a fit of madness, in unwarranted jealousy" ("And why the children?" "And what would have become of them without their mother?" "Ah, so you think it was to protect them, you think it was so they'd go with her?" "Not with her; with their grandmother." "Ah, okay, and why the old lady?" "That's why, and because she couldn't have borne the shame"), the irreproachable murderer had to have emerged from that room across the way that's closed now, and not just closed but blocked off by the plank across the door from one side to the other, and then to have gone in, full of mercy, first into one and then into the other of the other two rooms that are gazing out through their open doors, with a fogged-over absorbed look. I'm between the two, in the middle of the gaze. I move away. I step into the action. I enter on my own to intervene and witness from within my action so they won't carry me off to another action that isn't mine and that could be anywhere in time.

Naturally, I go quickly over to that room that can't be transposed from anywhere. I look through the eye of the keyhole. I don't see anything. Maybe there's another eye looking at me from the other side. Every time I spy through a keyhole the same thing happens to me. But if there were an eye here, whose would it be? No one's? A dead person's? They must have taken them away two years ago. Of course they are still here: everything that departs remains, and not in just one place like when they're here. Then what departs grows in all the corners, and what can no longer be there becomes all one. No one's. The eye must be no one's eye, or the eye of a solitude contemplating itself, although that would be worse.

I back off, walking backwards, and suddenly I go in there where Laura must be. She isn't there. Instead, I'm there, motionless, blurry, dressed just like Laura, in the wardrobe mirror. The unexpected apparition of that blue dwarf that has just discovered me makes me shiver. What if it weren't me? Or if I were there and not here? Well, it's not a question of beginning to make dangerous tests and beginning to change everything that's not here. I've got enough here with all these things that imprecisely denounce and hide what was here, enough with all this that can be barely perceived, a mere millimeter, revealing a nothing, and yet that's already enough so that someone always on the verge of being can be embodied and drag along a scene that came before this solitude, that must also have been contemplating itself with the eye of no one before I ever entered here. For example the empty bed, that's trying to pitch that folded mattress over the edge, where no doubt someone is being choked, was suffocated... And the bureau drawers, that are still trying to breathe for the last time... And the rocking chair, with its air of exasperation, if that wicker broken through by a fist and a clenched hand didn't indicate that... And the wardrobe capable of assenting, of consenting to anything, of hiding the evildoer without leaving a trace... No, no fogged mirrors that abduct me, that suck me right to the other side, where he may be standing. But out of the corner of my eye...

"No! No! No! No!" my voice goes spiralling down as my heart tumbles while I spin and crash and struggle against the arms of someone imprisoning me and leaning down and talking to me and—it's Miguel!

"Silly, silly Lía! Can't you see it's me? What's the matter with you?" while I sob on his shoulder in a stupid fit of weeping that shakes me and won't let go of me, although it fights me and pulls me back. "How come you didn't recognize me? Okay, enough now. There's no one there, see?" And he caresses my head and lifts it off his shoulder so I can see that there's no one there, no one other than Miguel who hugs me and I hug him, in the dim mirror in which that stranger appeared behind me just now.

Miguel looks at me worriedly, with a strained smile. He dries my tears with his handkerchief and takes me by the hand over to the mirror. He gets down on his knees beside me and wipes the tear-soaked handkerchief over the misty image of my face, over his misty face, until the two of us are inside a shining circle. (One more heaven rescued by my tears, not from my tears, like all the rest.)

There's Miguel: the lock of limp dark hair on his forehead, his eyes squinting a little, the color of hazelnuts with little dots of honey, his high cheekbones, his sharp pointy nose and his full teasing mouth. It's a mixture of other faces that would succeed it later, its features dispersed so I'd love them later on, when their time came, on other faces. Is it this image alone that I have to cut out again and share with other future images, or is it those others that I have to break apart and put together again piece by piece in order to remake this first one?

There I am: copper hair, green eyes that shift from bedazzlement to melancholy, a nose that decided, after a brief hesitation, to be straight, a wide mouth with its smile slumped a bit toward the left side. Is this the image that will be transformed several times, or is it the one that will make it to the end, recovered from all the reconfigurations?

"See? Did you think it was the bogeyman? I'm ugly but I don't scare anyone, no one but me anyway, and only when I'm going to bed, when I say my prayers and take stock of the day. Did you know your eyes seem just right for the king of jade?"

Jade makes my legs weak; it makes the back of my jaw shiver.

Miguel takes my face in his hands and stares right inside me. I don't know what he's looking for, I don't know what there might be deep in myself that he might find: an indecipherable inscription, a whirlpool that will suck him in, or a similar flash of lightning, maybe. Who am I talking about? Within me there are only tremors and a still unanswered question. I still don't know that the answer is another question. When I find that out I'll believe, no matter what the evidence against it, that affirmation is stamped like a seal onto eternity. Now the tremors are a closed beehive vibrating, a buzzing of a bumblebee trapped in a sealed container, and the question is so far from my lips, tangled in the threads of my ignorance, like a fish in deep waters. What am I missing? Where is the thing he's looking for? I lower my eyelids because I'm going to cry again over the ties that bind me, over my irremediable armored shell of innocence. I'm going to cry over my taste of nothing. Then I see the black silk necktie with silver stripes that dangles in two wide strips over his white shirt. That's what Miguel had just found and he was knotting it around his neck when I burst out: *"I see his face: so young, so brave, and already so hard. He'd gone back to pacing back and forth across the room when he began to unfasten that mysterious garment that wasn't his. It was strange to see him that way, in shirt sleeves, with his too-short pants and muddy shoes, unbuttoning that old-fashioned silk waistcoat that was part of a nobleman's wardrobe."** It seemed like a dream come to life.

"Can I tell you a secret if you'll forget it? I'm scared too, but I whistle, like this," and he whistled. (Miguel, I didn't forget your secret, but I can't remember your tune.) "Shall I tell you another secret if you won't forget it? Every night, before I go to sleep, I'm going to kiss your eyes in the hollow of my palm." (I forgot it until today, Miguel: I've only cried alone into the hollow of my palm.)

He kisses my eyes and goes off. (That mouth kisses me on a train as it leaves the miracle and goes off onto another face. Those eyes remain behind a door that I close forever, when they've left my eyes for another face. That lock of limp hair and that laugh both lie destroyed upon the face of a dead man.) He must have heard Laura's steps as she enters just

*From Henri Alain-Fournier, *Le grand Meaulnes,* published in France in 1913, about the romantic ideal, the search for the unobtainable, and the mysterious world between childhood and adulthood.

at the moment when I'm fastening the stone of need and desire around my neck, when I'm feeling that someday I'll have arms with which to fully receive and lose Miguel.

"What happened?" asks Laura, absent-minded and distant in the mirror.

"Nothing happened. I got scared. And what about you, what did you find?"—my voice scales up and down in incredible variations. I can't control it. It, too, is like a fish in deep waters that's having to cross through dangerously different temperature zones before it can appear again.

Laura looks at me a little surprised, but she's immediately absorbed in taking a quick inventory of everything she can see. (This room will go with me into other rooms. It will accompany me with my silence, my confusion, my ignorance and the unresolved mystery. Perhaps it's that unresolved ignorance through so many years that makes it—even now, when ignorance no longer exists and knowledge is an unresolved mystery—so that my love is ever tinged with unconquerable shame, as if I had to improvise an unfamiliar role. Maybe it's the feeling of a deception underlying all faith, or the insoluble crime that takes on another guise in the immolations of the future. Maybe that's the mirror where someone was, and can again be, an unknown person.)

"And what about you? What did you find?" I ask again from the roiling surface.

"A children's room. Nothing there. Just a mothball," says Laura and she disappears, because she's discovered, behind the door, another door that I hadn't seen.

I wait a second, but my anxiety doesn't go away. I'd like to have feathers to disguise what I'm hiding. There's no chance that I'll sprout them. I go out of that room wrapped only in my vulnerable skin.

The place Laura has found would be one to stay in if it weren't for all that could happen. It's no bigger than a balcony, and enclosed by transparent glass walls and all along them a row of red flowerpots, lumps of dried out soil and crumpled papers, hardened and yellowed. There's one with a bright spot on it that looks like a flower. ("Why are the begonias so red?" I'm asked sometimes in dreams by the same unknown old woman, as if it meant something much more, as if it meant to point out that someone or something dyed them. Even though there are no begonias here, if there ever were any.) There's an armchair of broken wicker, in front of a crate filled with jumbled papers. Laura picks some up, gives them a shake after skimming them quickly, covers the chair with them and settles in to investigate. I sit down beside her. There are old magazines, notebooks, pictures, postcards, several books in French—all covered with dust and spider webs and those sticky cottony residues that some insects generate to protect their undisputed solitude, and that perhaps seen through the unexplorable eyes of an insect look like marvelous tapestries.

L'Éducation Sentimentale, Gotas Líricas, a box of Doctor Andreu's Pills, a bottle of Guyot Solution, scenes of Mar del Plata in a hideous deathly green and "Our loving wishes to Mama, Norma and Oscar" on the other side, *Caras y Caretas* magazine with an energetic lady writing on a blackboard with both hands "Let's be ambidextrous," a notebook with the motto "Perseverance will be rewarded" that goes on to indicate that the sum of the angles of a triangle equals two straight lines, *Plus Ultra* with "A woman's weapons: a tortoiseshell comb, a swan and downy skin," and a Mrs. Dorrego showing off her terrifying dental plate in a big smile.

"What is jade?" I ask as if I had just read it.

"Where?" answers Laura, lost in the open parasols of "The Japanophiles of New York."

Where, what do you mean where? I don't know where. Anywhere: in "The land of the hyacinths," on the doorstep, on a garden bench, in the hollow of a palm. How should I know where? It's as if she answered me "When?" She's always asking questions like that. If you ask her "What time is it?" she'll answer "Why does it matter?" And if you ask her "Are you cold?" she'll say "For whom?"

"Anywhere. What is jade anywhere?" I answer patiently.

"Ah! Anywhere? One place is not like another. It changes." She's filling in time, trying to remember, while she goes on reading that Stomalix "gets rid of those nameless worries."

"Okay, here, in Toay, this afternoon."

"Oh well! In that case, it's that little green statue at home, in the case in the living room." And she closes the magazine with a slap, almost happily, stirring up a cloud of dust in the sunlight.

Now I remember. But I have to go back and look at it in order to know who I am with "eyes just right for the king of jade."

"All these people here are dead, but they aren't. It doesn't seem to me that they are. There were two children, a young woman and the grandmother. Do you see them?" asks Laura, as though she were trying to spot the victims in a labyrinth, hiding in the draperies with fountains and pillars in those photos where ladies and gentlemen look embalmed, with glass eyes, knees and elbows carefully bent, looking as though they're about to utter their last wishes or calmly pronounce judgments on aggressors, from a glass case.

"No. They aren't here." I say indifferently, coming back from another world. "The murderer must have taken them all away, to leave no traces," I add just to say something, though I already know that the murderer didn't worry about traces, that he even lit fires so he'd be found out.

"Silly"—that's the word with which Miguel's voice pinned me definitively inside my name, but she can't know that—"Silly. What do the photos have to do with the traces of the crime? You think he brought the photographer over to take pictures while he killed his wife, his mother and his sons, and that afterward he waited for the film to be developed and to get copies to take away with him? I'm talking about the pictures from 'before.' There couldn't be any others. But I don't see them," Laura continues with some impatience, while she digs around in the back of the drawer.

I take advantage of the moment to get up and leave, wrapped in the near ecstasy of my silliness. As I go by the room next door, I pause, I go over to the mirror, I leave a kiss on the cold dust, at the height where Miguel's face was, which as I step back is only my own image. Is my disappointment telling me that someday I'll know the aridity of true love: kissing my own image on the other's image? Or perhaps something much sadder: anxiously seeking the other only to find just myself in the end?

The closed door suddenly brings me back to awareness of where I am. Miguel's appearance yanked me from one tremor to another, from one dead end to another. But now that door embeds me again in a block of mystery where any displacement is inward, where any gesture bumps me up against the unsalvageable walls that surrounded me beforehand. I can't even forge ahead while I go down the steps, because all parts of this block are the same: a mass of bland, vibrating glass that moves along with me wherever I go. The only thing that can happen would be for someone to enter from some side or to become visible or be made manifest under the spell of a formula unknown to me that I may even be enunciating myself, unknowingly combining it with the rhythm of my foot as I move from one stair down to the next, and with this way of resting my hand on the railing. I have to fight against the horrible temptation of finding it. Nor can I go back. The part of this cube of terror that moves along in front of me pulls me slowly forward.

When I reach the bottom of the stairs, no one is there. Or everything is there in those dark pieces of furniture, dozing under the dust, in those dilapidated witnesses that enclose, just like the numbers hidden in a cipher, scenes and people who at any moment can disconnect from each other and recombine. It must be like putting yourself together again after a tidal wave of emotion has wiped you out, like unfolding a ribbon, like extending your wings outside this block that imprisons me together with danger.

I draw near the space under the staircase, seeking refuge in that pile of discarded fragments and ashes left there by a living hand that entered, left, and cannot reappear again because it still lights fires and leaves traces in another place. However, I don't have to hold too tight onto that hand, since I will eventually manage to make it coexist with me within the gelatinous transparency.

Then, as I turn my head I begin to see—this time in the cracked mirror of the living room—an unknown couple that surges up from the greenish depths of the stagnant waters and makes its way through an undergrowth of ferns and poisonous mosses, until they turn into Ruth and Miguel behind a glass. Ruth and Miguel blurry, eaten away by a fog of leprosy that gets thicker and falls, that hides and reveals one of Ruth's hands on Miguel's face riddled with holes, two worm-eaten faces that draw closer, overlap, and draw back again, a mass of dirty yellow hair that advances, covers the whole image and pulls it along with it in the tidal wave of this new shipwreck, back again to the depths of the waters that are closing over with a gleam of crystal smashed by this huge fist, put out by the resplendence of the ice melted by these tears.

Does this mean that I was not in the past but in the future? So this was the scene I was waiting for, the danger in disguise, the spell that would keep me trapped in this block in which I am definitively paralyzed in the same place? Will I ever again be something more than this small and trembling striation? Will I be able to grow beyond this insignificant shadow that contracts and folds into herself in an effort to disappear?

When Laura goes by, my face has just shed a fistful of tears. I hide a bit more while she dips into the dining room. Even more when she goes into the living room.

"And where's Lía?" Her voice sounds worried but doesn't stir me to move.

"I don't know. I don't think she came down." It's a sharp and indifferent tone, a metallic counterpoint of the full, caring, beloved voice.

Laura goes by me running. On the first steps of the staircase Miguel's footsteps catch up with hers. The boards are going to collapse. They're going to fall in, in a crash of splinters, of ceiling that is caving in on me, in this hell where the flames have been put out and all that's left is solidified air and wounds and shame. I hear them walk rapidly from one door to the next calling out to me in low voices, loud voices, waking who knows what ear with my name, murmuring hasty words. They go by over my head again at top speed. They keep on. They must have gone into the dining room. There's the sound of two chairs banging, and then the sound of a latch being shaken in vain.

When they go by again, I've almost decided to emerge: I'm almost able to move. But they go into the living room, and I still haven't finished packing away as much as I have to put away for later, and everything is happening too quickly.

"Didn't she come? She isn't anywhere." Why is she doing all this explaining to Ruth, who's barely even shaken her yellow-haired head to say no? "Let's look for her outside. She must have gone out," she adds with a hopefulness that moves me.

"She can't have gone out. We'd have seen her go by," says Miguel almost persuasively, but not too sure.

"But we never know how she vanishes or how she appears. She's capable of anything," Laura's voice answers with a certain pride, from farther away, mixed in with footsteps, with the violent scraping and the jump as she leaps out the window. Two more jumps.

I am alone in the house, with my name out there everywhere. It could happen now. It could all happen at once or someone might suddenly close the window. It would be better to get out right away, before I get trapped. Perhaps I can free myself from the air that closes me in. I try to move, and manage a little shift. Then I hear the noise. At first it is almost imperceptible: a light and cautious footstep. Someone is walking barefoot on the floor above. Going toward the staircase. The bare feet move slowly down, gliding over each step so they won't creak. They stop, fading into the silent complicity of the wood. Do they hear that I hear them? They continue. They move faster, weightless. With all the energy I can muster up, I hurl myself out of the place where I am, as though breaking almost invincible bindings or unsticking my glued-down skin. I think I can't run. But nevertheless, staggering, with weak knees and my feet snarled in the treacherous tangle of the invisible, I cross the living room, hoisted up by the vertiginous blessed expanse of the window, that sucks me in and disputes me with that force that hears me and sees me from everywhere, except from the color of Miguel, who appears I don't know how in the center of the light.

I jump and fall, turned into a pile of loose bones that almost put themselves together, uniting themselves miraculously while Miguel picks me up, while I say, before bursting into desperate sobs:

"There's someone there. I heard steps. Someone coming down the stairs. Let's go!"

Miguel holds me with one arm and extends the other toward the side I don't want to look at. How long does it take to close a window?

"There's no one there, Lía. Don't be silly. I just looked and I can tell you there's no one," he assures me very calmly and he begins to lead me down the same path we'd come up when we arrived.

I can't answer him "Exactly. There's no one there. There are footsteps, but there is no one." What's the use? Besides, I wouldn't be able to talk with these stupid spasms of this stupid crying that now Ruth can see, too. Because we've gone around to the front of the house, and there she is, indifferent as a log in the surface of this sunny afternoon, stirred up only by Laura's concern.

"What's happened? Where did you go?" She starts asking me before she comes over and then, while she shakes me gently by one arm so I'll answer her. "What happened?" over and over, at each unexpected turn, at the exit from any hell, that "What happened?" will become innumerable in Laura's voice, vacillating between desperation and the protective tone she assumes so as not to share my tears. "What happened?" How do I answer her now? How can I ever answer her?

"Let's go," says Miguel. "Leave her alone now. She'll tell you later."

We walk back through the tall grass. It's too exhausted to play the role of useless sentinel. No one asks it for permission to pass. It cannot warn anyone of danger's path. But it is friendly and crackles complainingly as we walk away. From time to time, a plume of grass lifts its head upward, terrified and incredible, indicating that it's still amazed at being viewed so continuously under the reverberating sun. Suddenly I rise up over its trembling vigilance and turn rapidly to gaze at the house with its look of looking beyond, with that insomniac fixedness in its amazement and in its transparent knowledge, with that lucid green that seems really "just right for the king of jade."

Behind one of the windows of the upper floor, the shadowy serious face of an old woman looms up between the fires and the broken flowers, fractured by the glass and the splendor of a summer day. The cottonwool head leans over the flames in a gesture of warning and of reprimand that includes by its end other paths within this path. "Why are begonias so red?" Perhaps they announce inexplicable crimes, perhaps vain profanation.

I don't say anything. Why should I? I always hear what no one said and see what isn't there. But my hand trembles uncontrollably, like a fluttering bird, imprisoned by Miguel's hand.

For Friends and Enemies

. . .

A yellow glow and nothing more. At one o'clock, all the lights go out. The glow submerges in the shape of a fish within my eye, and when the house is dark anything could happen: it could even begin to walk. It's possible that the house is already walking, slowly and majestically, with the night garden soaked in brilliant green, as if rising from the bottom of a pool. It puts on the bridal wreath and moves away. Or it's the black carriage that lurches off, urged along by the whistle of the dog pack or by the invisible coachman's lashing whip. Sometimes there's a cetacean upheaval and a long fissure opens up along one flank; it's just about to heave me over the edge in order to pass. At other times I feel a powerful crunching, almost calcareous, and I say to myself: it's pulling up its roots and going; and we leave, we would, that is, if it weren't because the crunching doesn't move from top to bottom, like bones being yanked up, but rather the opposite; it's more like a vaulted ceiling that's going to collapse onto the shaking pillars, that's it. And is this catastrophe that I'm inventing in order to distract the darkness any better than the inevitable appearance of the darkness itself? Wouldn't it be better if the shapeless thing crouched in the corner between the wall and the wardrobe just came out? Quick, a spell. I've forgotten that shapelessness is the worst. It could even be a chair with the head of a hippo, a loose veil that's blindly looking for me, the throbbing of a mollusk that's slowly devouring the room and furniture and Laura and all the rest.

Laura is asleep. Lately she's been whistling when she sleeps. Maybe she's afraid. Let's hope I don't start imagining that she could be transformed into a slithy tove or borogove, gyring and gambling in the wabe. Just as well. The door appeared, just in time. It began to appear little by little in another flash of light, because Grandmother strikes matches like little bones, lights the candles and begins to pray:

"For friends and enemies, for those I know and those I don't know, for the living and the dead. Enlighten them, dear Lord."

The flash of light is not enough. It only helps to not see or to see what would be better not to have there. The flash is the devil's pitchfork and makes things worse.

"For my grandmother, Florencia, to whom we all owe so much. And You, Lord, will repay these debts, even if You are unwilling, given her long memory, her careful planning, and her endless conniving."

Darkness is generous and has the foresighted memory of what it left yesterday and the day before yesterday. If I worked with it a little, we could compile an inventory of all the possible and impossible monsters of the world. Every night is a review extended by new combinations, by half lights that open like a trap so that something may emerge. And something always does emerge from the dim light cast over the darkness, from the dim darkness cast over the light.

"For my father, who sowed as many children as I know, not to mention those I don't know, children he will prefer not to acknowledge when You summon him, because he was forgetful and unless You've improved him, it will take a huge effort for him to recognize those who don't recognize him."

The monsters recognize me. That's why they come back every night. They crowd up close to me and I'm never entirely sure how many of them there are, because they are tireless in their metamorphoses. Sometimes I give them names in order to keep them straight, but they must lose those names with the light of day or else someone renames them, because sometimes the names repeat and even so, I don't know what they are called or whether they are the same monsters who come back.

"For my mother, who must be younger than I am and so I can oblige her to pray until her knees ache, like mine, because I'm no longer willing to pick threads out of the six threadbare trousseaus."

I begin to feel some cold pinches on my face, then I'm brushed by a little whisk broom and a ribbon flaps around my head. I wish I could fall asleep before they get here, fall asleep on this side, which is my great-grandmother's side. If only, with the last "Amen" of the Ave María, I could wrap myself up in these stitches, in these soft cottony clouds, fall into the chest where we keep the six great-aunts' sheets and tablecloths, smelling of apple, lavender, heliotrope, jasmine, rosemary, forget-me-nots, for never, for never and ever.

"For my sister Gertrude, who had as much patience as she had time for her worst acts, but all the best devices such as lies, cleverness and imagination; for my sister Cecilia, so that You will hold her in glory and alone, so she can't wake anyone, so nobody will have to help her clean, darn and mend everything You have to clean, darn and mend and even the little bit You may have left intact in this world; for my sister Eduviges: improve her complexion and her personality so she won't have to hide from or be embarrassed by anyone, and no one will have to hide from her; for my sister Valeria, and forget about her never being around when she was needed, except when she died; for my sister Viviana, although she never learned how to say thank you, even though she talked so much, and she was probably right about that; for my sister Patricia, let her beauty, indifference and stinginess turn out to be good for something."

Nobody is trying to cure me with this kind of icy ribbon around my head. These are not the ties of blood, and if they are, they may well be false ones. They'll probably drag me right now to the center of a ring where the six great-aunts are spinning and closing me up, all six of them with their hair loose and cold, all six of them the color of heavenly statues or faded earthworms. They'll probably tie me up and put me in a cage and keep spinning forever around me, in that naked garden where the wind blows. No ropes or ribbons, even if I have to defend my forehead with my hands all night long.

"For my four brothers, all of them womanizers and brave, so that at least they won't defy You while You're plunging them into hell. But before that, don't forget to review their achievements even though they may be wartime accomplishments and others that I can't name, because decency doesn't allow me to, and because I still have a lot to learn."

I'm not going to learn how to bear the night. The night's going to have to learn me, if it doesn't already know me thoroughly, because it has felt me all up and down and through and through my skin. It covers me with its smooth touch, it wraps me in blind bandages until it turns me into a larva, and it doesn't leave me a single bit of porous skin so I can breathe. It's better not to even try to move, on the verge of the namelessness already on its way. I don't know whether I could. And anyway, move what and to where?

"For my uncle Julián Ezcurra, cross-eyed, pro-slavery, and if You can't save him, oh Lord, don't worry about it because his bones would make a good fire for all those who have to burn with him, like his son Faustino, such a hard man no mortar could ever grind him."

If I could grind up that indeterminate creature that is approaching, breathing and slowing down purposely in order to torture me better; if I could chase it off with a powerful word I'll never manage to pronounce but that I feel exists somewhere; if only I could dissolve it in all the fears of the future, even if each grew a little stronger afterward, even knowing that they will also be intolerable when the moment comes. Get it over with; just devour me all at once.

"For my son-in-law Francisco, so that You'll reserve him a throne in this world, appropriate for the best man on earth, for everything You'll have to do for me to complete Your work. And don't come telling me that rewards are doled out later on, because then I'll answer You back that if You can't do it, then turn it over to some more powerful god, but get a move on, because I want to see and I'm impatient and in a pretty big hurry to die."

Now I'm going to start falling into something that isn't even death. It's a kind of inner vertigo. It begins with that taste of guts, with that over-fullness of my body, so alien and so evident, that I can't distance myself from it. It's too much substance for me, and I don't know where it is stitched to me or where I'm attached to it. And suddenly an abyss opens. A space opens between the two, as if what is outside were inside, and that's where I fall in, because I'm no longer contained in any way, because now it has forged an alliance with that other darkness that closes down and shoves me the opposite way. Where, where am I going?

"For my daughter Sofía, so generous and arrogant, as excessive in her kindness as in her anger. May You save her from tears and bitterness, and never make her hang her head in humiliation, in illness or in penury. But do lower her voice a little. And if You have time, teach her to be measured in her ways, but not using the stingy measures of others, because in that case it would be better for her to stick to her own."

And that's my mother, who, weeping or smiling, scoops me up from the bottom of any abyss, of this very one I was about to fall into, because she is my only reference in this world, my gate of knowledge or my wall of ignorance. That's my mother, who destroys the hurricane and keeps an ant from growing any bigger than its normal size. That's my mother, just like a decorated tower, a fortress covered with thorns, as grand as a cathedral and as tender as a candle's light or the brush of warm feathers on your heavy eyelids just as you fall asleep.

"For my daughter Lidia, who died so young. I'm not blaming You or asking You why. I'm as sparing of words with You as You were stingy with her future. I put her under the Virgin Mary's care, since the Virgin will know how to care for her better than You, and won't let her forget to starch her blouses and to put her paintbrushes in order, and to change the water in the vase of violets. And the Virgin will make sure to keep her bundled up well, because she's always been sensitive to cold and she went off in her nightshirt, leaving behind all the shawls and gloves and her brand new cloak she never got the chance to wear."

Heavy eyelids. No. I thought it was inside, but it's outside where it's starting to form, where what at first is a cloudy condensation is beginning to form, a mist that expands and takes shape and ends up being a woman. She's an old woman made of tulle and transparent fumigations. She always comes when Lidia is named, with time, with night, with fear and with patience. She dilates my eyes to enter, with a Viennese rocking chair, so she's there and not there.

"For my daughter Adelaida. Lord, I ask You fervently to perfect her, whatever it takes, even if it keeps her a spinster forever. Erase her without anyone noticing, and draw her again as I remember her: copy her from any picture of her taken at age seventeen, so that her face will again have the oval of a medallion, without anything extra, and her waist can be spanned by two hands, and the rest in the most perfect molded shape, so that she can once again wear white organdy or red velvet. And if that isn't possible, go back twenty years, even though those of us here now are no longer all of those who were here then."

All right then. Now she is completely formed. She sways, as light or as diffuse as if she were poised on a tuft of cotton in bloom or were a prisoner in a stormy winter windowpane. Tomorrow they'll tell me not to be scared, that it's just great great grandmother Florencia, who died fifty years ago. But I can't look at her as though she were a picture. And anyway, no picture arrives on its own. And what if she suddenly came closer? I'll bet Laura is looking at her, too. It's better not to take your eyes off the disappeared when they've appeared, because it's impossible to know what they've come with or what they'll carry off with them. Without losing sight of her, I reach over to Laura's side of the bed and immediately feel her hand, which has reached out for mine. That's how it always happens.

"For my grandson Alejandro, who died at twenty. You know why You did what You did. It's useless to try to excuse Yourself by telling me that God picks the chosen ones, because You would be obligating me to pray for the perversity of those who remain. He was handsome; he was intelligent, noble, and saintly. Didn't You have enough angels and archangels in your court? Did You really need one more? I tell You this face to face, without humility or resignation: You and he will share the right hand side of God the Almighty Father, and even then who knows if You can count on my forgiveness."

Laura's hand is warm, moist and trembling. And what if this isn't Laura's hand? I glance over, even though Great-Great-Grandmother Florencia might seize that moment to move toward us, rarefied, rocking forward irrevocably in her chair. The vague shape that is Laura looks like any nighttime condensation: an immense insect with folded wings that will suddenly jump, a drowned woman who floats on her bed of ensnarled vegetation, a ship's prow ready to sink me into the depths. I try to let go of the hand, but it imprisons me with a shared strength of desperation.

"For my granddaughter María de las Nieves, with so many sufferings awaiting her and so few gardens with masked guests and strung party lights, which is what she likes best. She will marry young, to a man with the gaze of a tiger and a sentimental heart, a blend of wild beast and dove. Let her complexion be protected, and her joyfulness sustained. May she have many children because our family name ends with her. Make it continue under other names and in other memories, so that we are recognized, and let nobility and truth be exalted above all else."

It must be that my own hand is inventing another hand, my own blood projected out to defend or aid me. No, and perhaps yes, because I hear Laura's voice speaking softly, just like the tone she uses to discuss the date, or sicknesses or eclipses, which is almost the template of her identity: "Lía, do you see her? Are you seeing her?" "See who?" I ask, fearful that she isn't referring to the same thing. "Her. Who else would it be?" "Yes, I see her. What do you think she'll do?" "Anything." "What do you mean anything?" "Anything except rock herself back and forth." "But that's exactly what she's doing." "And do you think that's what she came for?" "I don't know. Maybe she forgot something." "And what if we gave her the box of paintings, and Lidia's clothes and the skeleton that's in Alejandro's room?" "Wouldn't it be better to ask her what she wants?" "No, don't you see she's already leaving?"

"For my granddaughter Laura. Now she is lovely and wild, especially when she whinnies or makes a rabbit face. That has its appeal. But I want her to be like a holy image, lit up inside and out. Fix her up, Lord, and encourage her lack of concern so that it will turn into a concern for the welfare of others, encourage her indifference so that it will become passion when it is needed; encourage her excessive way of being, so that no one can feel alone when her name is invoked."

"Grandmother Florencia, go away," I mouth the words and blow them toward her without making a sound. And great-great-grandmother goes off trotting on her misty cloud, passing through the window blind, invisible now, no doubt going on to become part of the foggy assembly forming on the other side, because now I can hear whispered exchanges, deadened hoof beats, a soft rebound against the walls. They are falling from the sky in swarms. Can't you hear something spinning like a windmill of huge feathers brushing and tapping on the peephole?

"For my granddaughter Lía, timid and prone to melancholy and withdrawal. Make her able to hold something in her hands that are the hands of the dispossessed. Out of her weaknesses, create a strength. Remember that she nearly died when she was a year old and so may have left much of her life in another place, outside of this world. Return this life to her at least in intelligence, in faith and in charity, because I greatly fear that there is nothing to be done about her hope. And I don't even ask You to grant her beauty, because it wouldn't be any good to her."

I can only hope that this sound of brushing growing louder and louder against the blinds ends at once. It spins with an ever more powerful banging, sounding more and more urgent. "Laura," I whisper at the moment I feel that the entire house is going to start walking, lifted high by this wheel of wings. But Laura is asleep again, clutching the bedrail in that grasp that is so hard to pry loose, unless she lets go of it herself. "Laura," I go on insisting anyway, on the verge of flight, almost moving now.

"For myself, who am nothing, but who should be the last to die so that no one can weep for me."

Someone's here. It's better to know someone's here. I get out of bed and move forward trying to brace myself strongly on this floor that rocks back and forth as it ascends, that's going to pitch me to one side or the other. Breathless, I reach for the window blind, the fragile barricade against the unknown. Where can I find the strength to open the peephole? Without moving, I look first toward the glow, toward the open door, toward the bed where Grandmother is engraved, almost phosphorescent against the pillows, a little more solid in body, a little more tenacious than her grandmother Florencia.

"What's going on, sweetie? Where are you going? Why aren't you asleep?" she asks with a voice that is like a strong current of air.

"There are noises, Grandmother. Don't you hear them?" I say, trying to form a countercurrent that will bring us together and serve to reject what's outside.

"Yes, I hear them. Go back to bed and don't worry. Sleep. Those are just the ghosts, nothing but ghosts."

Heads or Tails

. . .

I.

"See me, Mama? Are you sure you see me, or do you just think you're seeing me because I see you and I think you see me?"

"I see you. You can be sure that I can see you," and she leaned her face over close to mine and we stared at each other until her enormous black eyes slid together, overlapped and merged, fusing into a single immense cyclop's eye, made up almost entirely of pupil, very alive and vibrant, where no doubt, if I'd looked closer, I'd have seen the whole past, present and future of the world go by, wrapped in the glow of compassion and tenderness. But Mama broke into the game with her laugh, and I laughed, too, a laugh more like an unsteady nervous giggle.

Mama, you thought it was a shared game. You didn't realize that it was a solitary game, that I felt all alone in a world where every answer was a projection that came out of me, went forth and embedded itself in one of the walls that closed me in. Even time itself, the remote past, was something I was ignorant of simply because I'd forgotten about it in the face of overwhelming eternity. Austerlitz, Greek columns, the martyrdom of Saint Catharine, sealed into their picture frames were, just like you, the sky and the weasel, a minute fraction of my presence in the world. The insurmountable centuries, the unknown distances, and the infinite combinations of everything nearby that I could begin to imagine—all of these terrified me equally. It was all part of me and I was foreign to myself, transferred into another self that I assumed in my ignorance. It was then that I'd refer to myself telling you about "her," since the "you" with which you answered me did not suffice to split the world into at least two parallel worlds. But you'd take on the "her" referring it to yourself, and again you'd leave me totally alone. Over the course of years I can testify that God can't be happy, and not exactly because of sin; perhaps on the contrary, He's got the sensation of being accompanied. Maybe every horrible proof is nothing more than the apparent freedom that arises from His dissatisfaction and His protest. I just know there's some innocent trick to all this, set up to look like a mistake, and it's a displacement of command, of powers. I seem to not have His Sacred Will on my side. Yes, what did He create us for? And why did He create us like this? Exactly. He created us in order to be able to see His imperfections, in images, in awkwardness, in order to perfect himself. And He divided himself up so much among us all, that He's probably not in a single place anymore, outside of us; He'll probably turn back into himself, happily, when each of us becomes what He wanted for his united self. We probably use up, by living it, the trace of evil that dissatisfied Him. Then He can probably get back to recovering His unity, much improved. I have no idea why.

But now I know that you weren't only in me. If it had been that way, you wouldn't have left. It's this forthright evidence against my very existence that makes me ask you again:

"Mama, do you see me? Are you sure that you see me?"

II.

It's possible that the "invisible" game was a continuation of that first one, since it was a way of standing back from the world, of turning it into an unfamiliar object by viewing it.

(I should clarify that I was ignorant of the most elementary anatomy. The references to the body as "a bag of shit" made by someone who bellowed it from a "shithole" high in a pulpit, plus some definitions stumbled upon by chance in the big *Dictionary of the Language,* where it talked about "low and imperfect nature" and of the "evil vices" that corrode the soul, had discouraged me from any closer acquaintance of any kind.)

To play "invisible" you don't need potions or formulas or ceremonies. You can play it anywhere, anytime. You only need to focus your mind, letting the air move through you freely. I took a deep breath with my eyes closed. I turned that vibrant transparency into a central deposit and then dispersed it out in all directions, right through my skin. The invaded zones shrank back inside, in a receding tide of color, retracting in inverse motion. I'd expel them when I breathed out, not in substance, but in a gust of varied tones—blue, red, gray, white—that would combine into random shapes without outlines. Sometimes they were only arabesques and mosaic patterns. But once I pulled a white tapestry speckled with blue fish out of myself; another time, I managed to extract an amazing rainbow. I don't even want to remember Chinese shadowplays, tentacled splotches, processions of ants, or disturbing chessboards.

I never thought about clothes, either. Stepping up the allusive rhymes, I no doubt assumed that they were contaminated by the very essence they contained. So that once transparency was achieved, I could circulate, blending in with the atmosphere. I've passed time this way at weddings, funerals, family councils; I've blown out candles and I've grimaced at venerable people from my transmuted form as an errant breeze, and I really think that nobody ever saw me, although some perceptive person may have peered at me once or twice. Or could there be some big conspiracy that favored me, an order that opened up in huge silent circles and included that period of time when I thought I was crazy or had involuntarily disappeared or was in the midst of odd ongoing metamorphoses? To ask it is to leave the game or to violate the rules of a generous complicity.

Well, all right, then afterward it seemed enough to inhale and reabsorb my occasional inner drama, slowly and in detail, and then I'd reappear again in a distant place, because I took care—maybe out of modesty—to do this well away from all gazes. Meanwhile, where might my spurned contents, my dense and corporeal displaced zone, have wandered? At some point, someone must have seen that unlikely array of tapestries, hanging from a tree or stretched out over a wall. Someone could have destroyed me without even knowing it was a crime.

It never happened to me. Still, I have the impression that at some point I couldn't manage to precisely recall a series of complex yellow geometries. If that was so, everything else has just been an error. I don't even want to think about it. But why am I overcome still now by that vision of a golden city, so much like the City of the Caesars, that I saw many years later, as it crossed through the sky, wrapped in a cloud?

III.

There's also the game of "being somebody else." It's a game to play at odd hours, when the persistent repetition of one's own name, chanted in a low voice, slowly, turns into a hammer that, when skillfully manipulated, pounds the self into fragments. The self starts out by spinning and shrinking, concentrated by the centripetal force of fear, until it looks like a woody fruit the size and shape of a nut. It slips by and turns, hides under the curtain folds that hang within us from head to toe. When you've figured out the exact hiding place, you hold out a moment, to build anticipation of discovery or to give the hider an illusion of being totally safe. Then you say the name again, even slower, in a scandalized tone of profound scolding and surprise. The self looms up, impelled by the need to justify itself, and that's the moment when you strike the final blow. It should be precise and definitive so as to avoid useless mutilations or surviving zones of blame and protest, which would interfere later with the freedom to act. (The process is noticeably shorter if it takes place by candlelight, inside a closet, or with one's head hidden under the sheets.)

But wait a minute. The game doesn't end there.

The second part requires a mirror. I had one on my bureau. No. There was one on the bureau ("*I*" and "*my*" no longer exist). No one stood in front of it and in the candlelight contemplated that face distorted from the mold of a shape and a color; those terrified eyes that were someone else's. From the seedbeds of fixed ideas, or rather, from the cellar of past incarnations—that rise to the surface even when the current incarnation bursts through the surface of its waters, that is, when the rupture of the self occurs—then a name would emerge, another name, as insistent as the previous one. With difficulty, it opened a passage through the rubble, groped its way along dim corridors, and tangled itself in the thick hangings. It pressed forward almost on its back side, like a ship weathering a storm, or like a house that's sinking, but it kept advancing until it pulled itself arduously through a long slim crack set between the clenched teeth of the rock. It loomed up, weak and exhausted, after the difficult journey: "Matrika Doléesa."

Matrika Doléesa had taken over the territory where her name was proclaimed. The name was now the tenacious weapon that pounded unremittingly against unknown matter. Percussion invaded the inner ear of consciousness. It surged in a maddening drumbeat accompanying the ceremony. Meanwhile the face of a savage queen loomed out of the smoke that fogged the mirror. Skin white and tautened by the transparent porcelain of the mask, the eyes dark and stormy beneath strained lids, a crown of branches on the foliage of overgrown hair, and the stiff, flat and gleaming mouth that had just closed upon the last recently pronounced syllable, Matrika Doléesa concentrated on the restrained tension of the leap that would pull her into the ritual dance and hence to sacrifice. Her feet felt elastic, expressive and as sensitive as her very hand clenched around the black stone knife. Expectation wove its plot into a network of threads of blood. A few more drum rolls and there'd be a feline leap onto her prey, a tiger wrapped in a lightning bolt that would suddenly unfold into a ribbon of luminous perversity. A salty taste, a taste of rejection burbled up from the buried springs of memory overflowing my mouth, halting me at the verge of that downward leap. I began again to name myself in a low voice, very slowly, until the persistent repetition turned into a hammer that, when skillfully manipulated, pounded the self into fragments.

I could unearth other heroines, well known or not, who leapt either horizontally or upward: Griska Soledama, sad orphan, who endured all the trials of displacement in inclement weather; Darmantara Sarolam, in whom all names converge, all threads of destiny from a carriage whose wheels are two suns. I could also summon the first little nut, miraculously restored, make it roll along and grow within me, pulled along by the uncontainable current of this name I will never manage to inhabit.

Sometimes I have the feeling that I've indefinitely prolonged the order of the game: at other times, I think a mistake was made, some involuntary exchange produced by my haste when I heard unexpected footsteps; but most often I feel that the first I—that is to say, the last one—failed on some occasion to return intact, that there was a slip up, a crack that continued to permit someone to burst through as a surprise, when I least expect it.

IV.

In some way "the antipodes" is a more social game—though not exactly a parlor game—if it is compared to others that are purely solitary. It started out, no doubt, as a personal interpretation of the law of gravity and of the magnetic pull between the Magdeburgian hemispheres, plus the fantastic element—borrowed from I don't know which story—of a double who awaits us in another century or on the moon.

I never understood clearly whether this person was identical, analogous, or complementary. When I wanted to think about it, it was already a fact: human conduct and movement had been locked for me into an unprovable theorem: "The power of opposing doubles holds us together." In other words, the inhabitant who is located on the opposite place on earth is held in place, and I'm held here, thanks to the mutual force of attraction that is beamed from our bodies and could be drawn as a line from his heels to mine,—and vice versa—passing through the center of the earth. When he moves, I move; when I jump into the sea, he jumps, or falls, into the sea; when we travel, we travel in opposite directions in order to remain in the same balanced relationship. Could you ask for a more separated synchrony, a less opposed opposition? Our gestures are simultaneous reactions to each other and our acts engage us in a total complicity (how could we perform different actions but have identical gestures?). Of course we can't know who threw the first stone, since each of us is throwing simultaneously, but you can tell when the motive is one's own or the other's by the level of apathy or engagement with which the acts are begun and carried out. And don't go thinking that I'm using this to dodge responsibility or avoid blame and punishment. I've never said: "He made me do this" as others do who appear to be unaware of the theorem, although sometimes, really, I've been on the verge of exclaiming: "Come on! Hey! Where are you going, with nothing stopping you?"

Well, the fact is that at the very moment when I closed myself up in my room, he, "the antipode," must have been closing himself into his. I moved one foot slowly. I stopped. I took a few steps. I bent my ear down to hear the crash that must be happening in the center of the earth (eventually I discovered that an echo is nothing other than this kind of crash); I gave a leap, and continued to perform complicated gymnastics that were shamefully exaggerated and that I recall now with remorse. Once, for example, I hung from a lamp, balancing as on a swing, and I gave a great mortal leap onto the empty bed, shouting: "Follow this, if you can." I split my head open against the edge of the nightstand. Now we have the same scar, a pale reminder that comes to life in big storms. Of course, he got even, and how!

Despite everything, I know I would have loved him. It's such a shame! Our love could have been the only indestructible one. It breaks our hearts to think that we'll never meet either on this side of the earth, or on the other. We can only try out loves that begin as though we had been able to meet, loves that cause us to lose our sense of gravity, and hurl us into the air like angels, up to great heights. But the lover we have sought doesn't follow us. Restricted to the law of bodily attraction, he is unfamiliar with the rules of the antipodes and remains on earth or heads off in an unknown direction, carried along by universal attraction. This ending is somewhat similar to our permanent situation. It's so sad!

There are no more than two solutions:

One would be to get hold of an 180° angle that's just beginning to close irrevocably, but whose sides allow us to cling to it as we move closer to each other, until one day we manage to enclose ourselves between its resistant walls with no exit possible. But isn't this what usually happens to all couples?

The other solution I mentioned, which is the one I prefer, that we prefer, would be to dig down until we find each other in that igneous mass, in that nugget of fire buried in the depths of the globe, and burn, burn in a mutual fire until the same flame consumes us both.

The Tamarisk Hedge

. . .

A key opens a panel in the wall. It's the same key that opens wide the doors of insomnia so that distant cities appear, unknown travelers, carriages, epidemics, and shipwrecks that invade the space where I am. But those who visit me most often are people and maps that resemble a piece of my destiny.

Now the wind slips in through a great crack in my hideout. And now desolation enters in the form of a prairie, retracting its arid skin like an animal pacing in circles before settling. Because I've grown, but the desolation has grown alongside me, day after day, at the expense of my bones, at the expense of the walls of the present. It was never banished to the farthest corner among the discarded junk. It was never denied its sweetest holocaust: the shady garden with damp herbs, the hedge of tamarisks forever enclosing a crumbling fortress, every inch claimed by nettles and scorpions; the rarest snowfall and its ringdove of smoke whispering forgiveness from above; Grandmother's saints in their blue glass case; my sisters' arbor where bees buzz in a double rainbow of sweetness and patience. Insatiable, unquenchable, this plain. And yet the prairie rocked me to sleep with terrors, mysteries, and legends, leaving me with a thirst greater than the cup filled to the brim with all that remoteness.

A hand made of sand slowly caresses the measureless distance that reaches up to my pillow. A hand turned pale by the dead half moon in the lap of ever-shifting dunes. If it rained, each drop would be eagerly consumed, would sink into some underground sediment that holds my talismans made of little stones, bird bones and seeds carved with enigmatic signs that I try to decode with my own life story. What a priceless treasure for archeologists of the future!

But it doesn't rain. Saint Rose does not pass by like the chosen one with a great cloud floating across her forehead, nor does Saint Barbara toss her sparks and lightning bolts into the well. September does not drag along its cape of yellow butterflies, nor does November cover us to the point of suffocation with its somber cloak of locusts.

Only the wind, that deluded god who entwines his crowns with rusted branches and thirsty leaves, moves forward through the underbrush with his cortege of survivors. He is an excessive god that you can't even forsake. I've seen him dragging fatal migrations, entire colonies that seemed to represent the fall—not downwards, but toward the east. The faces of those people were shaped with a tough, resistant substance; their expressions and even their clothing had a look of finality, as if they were passengers prepared to spend years in a station waiting room until they heard the whistle of a train that would only leave them in another, identical room. I see the line of carts on the road, with their useless umbrellas, their blue washbasins and their wardrobes whose mirrors cast a gleam of goodbye, a despairing flash across the walls of the houses that still have no neighbors. I toss sunflowers at them when they pass, and I watch them, I watch them as they disappear through the eye of the needle, into the other side.

On this other side it's still the hour of the siesta and we have to climb down from the tree of green fruit, from the tree of knowledge where we're hiding like the little animals in the tapestries, and run from La Solapa, the cruel lady of the sun, who dresses like an iguana and comes out to chase children who wander or sleepwalk. If she catches them, she turns them into dwarves with huge straw hats and outfits made out of tattered vegetation. The son of Lady Lora (the beggar woman who lives in a cave) was allowed to grow, but she kept him in a caterpillar's cocoon. Lora goes from door to door crying plaintively, "A big coin for Lady

Lora!" and she flees with a weasel's steps to hide in her underground den. I suspect she shares her quarters with La Solapa. They have identical hats.

Our spy organization will figure it out some day. My spy badge says "GKY," which means God Keep You, and I am only a level 4. The other kids are older and have a higher rank. Some of them aren't afraid to investigate anything, at any time of day. Not even death, which can tumble from a passing train at midnight and chase after the one who saw it. It can—just like the Russian thistles, those moving masses that get bigger and bigger as they roll, till they become a jagged ghost that devours the evening fires one by one, that devours the storm and me inside it, with Grandpa Damián on horseback in the night of utter misery, when we're on our way back from Telén and my brother Alejandro isn't here anymore, and where he was has become all sobs and cracking ice among black clothes—but all of that is one leap they won't let me take with everyone else.

I see it. I see the house that always starts moving at night, slowly and majestically, dragging in its wake the garden, the cottages and the mill, displacing the occupants who have traded my blood for their ticket to travel. Mama, Papa, Grandmother, Aunt Adelaida, Alejandro and my sisters—Laura and María de las Nieves—play at being the passengers of eternity, each in a golden chair, each in a role marked by Providence, by power, by mercy, by bewilderment, by absence, by complicity, by adventure. The house rocks, it sways, it tips, listing to one side as if trying to toss overboard all the passengers with their furniture and their trunks. I'm not afraid, because it's up to me. I was the last to arrive, and I'll stay behind to turn off the lights when no one else is left, when they've all turned into the kings and queens of solitaire.

Even later, this wandering house that I bump into everywhere will keep appearing, called forth by every summer, by every full moon, because solitude remembers everything and cries out for ghosts and missing persons and makes them visible. Solitude is garrulous and it displays all its belongings under the sun of total darkness. It lingers over a man, over a wheel, over a shadow, over some bones that will kindle their good lights in the night; it sets them apart and displays them and raises them up to the sky like the angels of its own annunciation. The solitude of the plain is located in the center of the world. You can see it from anywhere.

There stands the child that I was, the one who tried on, among other masks, this face that I now wear. She hasn't been able to bequeath all her possessions to me. Many fireflies have gone out; many bits of frost of the kind that once shrouded clusters of flowers at dawn have dissolved in a pool of water where I no longer see myself. But the heavenly emissaries, those who composed their language with signs culled from mystery, from the nostalgia of another paradise, leave in the middle of this room a burning chest where the cadaver of innocence lies intact.

Come forward, guardians. Encarnación, the white witch with chicken hands and blue woolen tights, embodied in the eagle of her spells, pours the mineral veins of my fever onto a piece of marble and so stops death. Queen Guinevere comes barefoot, wrapped in scraps of silk and lace, with a necklace of glass beads that gets longer from town to town and a fan that won't open because it's covered with signatures that testify to her madness. She blows on my eyes so I'll never cry. Nanni, the frustrated opera singer, with his white gloves and shabby frock coat of rat-colored green, cheapskate green, traces with a spoon the circle that separates him from the earth, and ascends the stairway in the granary that leads to the Final Judgment. All three of them have a wing in the middle of the back, a brittle wing that's crumbling into dust. It falls over my face in a slow whirlwind that sucks me upward from there beyond, from forever, from the place where darkness is another sun, and it transports me to here, to now, where the light is also an abyss.

Queen Guinevere blew on my eyes so I wouldn't cry. "Don't cry, never cry, Josefina," she said. Queen Guinevere lied.

Solferino

. . .

One morning I looked out the window, and there they were. The night before they had set up camp, among the weeds and sunflowers, in the lot across the street. I saw the tents with colors swarming around them, tinged with the black of bluebottle flies. I knew it was them. Although I'd never seen them before, for me they held the intense attraction of legend and mystery. The men were dressed in dark colors, maybe in black, and they wore black hats. The women wore long flower-printed skirts with blouses and headscarves in every color, but especially the deep purplish-red solferino (fierce sun, ferocious sun, savage sun). I was convinced that's what "solferino" meant when a few days later I saw three of the women up close, with their dark, bushy eyebrows, those spider-eyes that move and stop quickly, the dark sparkling of the skin accentuated by many moles, the stiff braids, the strange movement of their hips—not from side to side, but up and down—and that majestic and irrevocable walk that threatens, that comes close, that encroaches and steps over the line. The step of a shoe with a metal buckle, red shoes, heel-clicking shoes. A step as dangerous as fate. "Don't go near them, girls!" "Even if they call to you and offer you little colored stars, run away." "Be careful—they steal children and sell them!"

So they steal them! Couldn't that be the secret of my birth? The reason behind those uneasy moments, the exchange of glances and even the whispers that linger behind me every time I ask who brought me, how it happened, where I came from? I don't like the answers they give me, stuff like things about roses, or cabbages, or big ugly birds, which don't explain anything—and especially that story that María de las Nieves tells: that Laura and I are dwarves, that we were born from an Easter egg hatched by Felicitas and Chico Dick, the circus dwarves. It's not that I want to be the daughter of kings and queens or of mysterious princes that you may never find, and who might be cruel and horrible anyway, and who have warts and live in perpetually cold countries. I'd just as soon have Papa and Mama. Besides, I love them. But who hasn't tried out in childhood, and even much later in life, two or three different destinies? So when I tried on the crown and glided through the great halls of golden mirrors and tapestries of crimson velvet, everything sounded hollow as ice and smelled like closed-in darkness, and I was afraid. I went back to the living room of our house and I hid.

The living room was splendid, and would always be splendid. But I couldn't live my whole life without knowing. I kept a closer watch. I should confess that more than once I misinterpreted certain allusions or half-heard words, like this very morning when Mama and Grandmother were talking about "those dirty people that take advantage of you if you don't watch out" and about "those two innocent creatures, victims of their intrigues." Just when I was thinking that those two were Laura and me, I learned that they were talking about two turkeys that had disappeared overnight. Anyway, one had to discover the truth.

That's what my mother said, obviously referring to turkeys and the thieves. And that afternoon, when I saw Imaginaria leaving the house with a bundle that probably held casserole dishes and pots, I figured out where she was headed and—though I was forbidden to—I followed her.

Imaginaria always seems like a scared animal, caught in the moment of her greatest terror, with her hair on end and her wide eyes fixed on who knows what vision. As soon as she discovered that I was following her, she stopped, I stopped, she spun around, she shook herself like a tree shaking off the rain, stomped on the ground and yelled, "Go back home! Home!"—pointing with a stiff index finger like those signs with little hands pointing in the direction you should take.

She turned around again. She took a few more steps and so did I. She stopped, I stopped. We repeated the whole operation three or four times, until she had arrived, and I had arrived as well, because I was smart enough to catch up with her little by little. I also figured that she would stop in front of the only wall that fronted the vacant lot. It was one of the four walls of an old abandoned shed, maybe what remained of a larger structure whose purpose nobody knew. Until two weeks ago it had been the supposed hideout of the "old man with the sack" or the outpost of all the delinquents, adventurers or redeemers born of the imagination. Since then, somebody had placed a flimsy door in the hole of the entryway and had stuck there a wordy sign, in green letters on a white background: Club of the Programmaticals. Who could the "Programmaticals" be? Maybe those seven or eight guys I saw from my window, who came from all directions and arrived at this door every day at six in the afternoon? I don't even know if they were always the same ones. None of them wore a badge, and I would see them go in, but never come out.

Now I stood stock still, a few feet from Imaginaria. She gave an angry shudder. With her blonde hair standing on end, she looked like a giant nettle. She shouted, "Don't move! Stay right there! Go back home, now!" And she shook her arm and hand as if trying to shoo away some pesky creature.

"I came on my own. Nobody gives me orders, not even the Great Merlin or the King of France, because I'm not anybody's secret messenger," I answered resolutely.

She swallowed hard, measuring her response, but at that very moment the door opened.

"Who are you looking for?" asked the boy with a nice smile who stood there. He had great shining dark eyes and he was wearing a tall pointed hat made of black cardboard and a gray cloak, which might have been a tablecloth, sprinkled with strange figures in many colors.

"Are you the tinker?"—Imaginaria's voice sounds uncertain, shaky, too thin to conceal what she's got hidden.

"No, I'm Juan the Alchemist, or Juan the Magician, as you like. Come in."

She steps forward and I slip in behind her, close on her heels. Juan the Magician, he said—and had I not just named Merlin the Magician? I have always performed, and always will, this sort of useless miracle.

"The guy who repairs pots and pans is Joaquín. He's over there—" the young man explains politely, pointing toward the back through the gap of a nonexistent door. "Go ahead. You'll recognize him right away because he has a flame in his hand."

"A flame in his hand, a flame in his hand," Imaginaria repeats, walking and swinging her bundle and murmuring like someone possessed, "A flame in his hand, a flame."

I don't dare to follow her or to stay where I am. This place is strange. It seems like an ordinary room, but it's not. It has no roof, the walls are crumbling, there's a dirt floor and in the middle stands a tall tree with flimsy limbs and shiny leaves. So shiny that in the middle of all that ruin it seems like a newcomer, although it looks less like an intruder than like the boss of the situation, keeping an eye on everything, keeping an eye on me. It didn't frighten me because I didn't think about hail or lightning, but rather about a possible place for birds, clouds, and angels to stop and rest. Later I remembered that the heavenly spirits aren't the only ones who know how to fly.

"Aren't you going with her, with the sleepwalking lady? Didn't you come in together?" asks Juan, not smiling, leaning on some shelves made of cases where I see different sizes of bottles with all kinds of liquids, powders, and pills.

"Yes, but no," I say, trying to hide behind the tree. Then I add, on an inspired whim, stammering, "I came for another reason. I came to join the club, the club of the cool guys."

"I should have known it by the look on your face. But here there's no cool guys' club. The cool guys come here to eat. You'll have to start that club if you want one. But come out here, let me see if you have hair on your lip," he answers mockingly.

I screw up my courage and ask, "What about the Club of the Programmaticals?" with a voice as big as an ant's.

"Oh, that's what you meant! The Programmaticals' Club is a secret of mine. I already told you I'm Juan the Alchemist. This is my laboratory." And he gives me a look of Olympian superiority. His mouth is a slash of smugness as he explains: "Besides mixing substances, I'm looking for an order—a programming—of letters, words, and numbers that will unlock the keys of every mystery. That's why I call it the Programmaticals' Club: pro-grammaticals. I'm the only member so far, but that's enough."

I'm looking at him dumfounded, probably open-mouthed, as I come out into the open. This gypsy is too changeable. His face shifts from seduction to scorn. It's like what happens with dice: you don't know if you'll roll a two, or a six, or a one. And on top of that, he's a magician, but he doesn't know anything. He doesn't know that I'm looking for the same thing he is, that when I'm alone I combine little stones, seeds, even tea cakes and sugar cubes at breakfast with the same intention: to the right, to the left, up, down, one, two, three. He doesn't know it's the same reason I'm starting to combine words. He doesn't know I'll keep combining them all my life, until now, when I'm able to return to that time from every direction in order to tell it.

He smiles to himself, sympathetic but contemptuous, stuck in his ignorance, and adds the final touch: "Why am I telling you this, little girl? You don't know a thing."

"I do so! Of course I know—I do it too!" I say, infuriated, my self-esteem in flames, and I throw myself as fast as I can, with skidding, stumbling steps, forwards and backwards, into the tangled territories of my enigmas and my searchings, until I emerge from a sudden short cut into the lonely crossroads of doubts about my family origin.

During all these criss-crossings, the face of Juan the Alchemist stayed with me in its countless variations like a kaleidoscope, only more expressive in his apparent enthusiasm, in his disapproval, in his acquiescence, in his pretense of interest. At times he took my undisciplined words and put in the right ones, and he urged me protectively to go on each time I was about to give up.

When I finished talking, with my expression shifting one way and another, we were almost friends.

"Please, help me find out. Maybe somebody in your family knows something," I said at last. I knew that directly accusing someone of kidnapping was wrong. I also felt terribly guilty about doubting my parents.

"I'll help you. I swear by your shadow, by your eyes, by the light that shows you the way. I don't think my family knows a thing, and it's almost certain you are your parents' child. Me too, I thought I was the son of King Solomon, of Rasputin, of Mata Hari, even of the way my great uncle said hello—and you see, none of that, I'm the son of my parents."

By this point we felt like true friends. Maybe because of the trust he placed in me when he confessed he was "the son of his parents," or because of the generous oath he swore for my shadow, my eyes, and my light.

The instant he continued talking, though, we started growing apart quickly. They would leave the next day, and I could go with them as his assistant, we would leave before 7 a.m., heading for points unknown, I'd have to be there at 6:30, with all the money and valuables I could find, and I shouldn't say anything to anybody or who knows what might happen.

His tone went from cajoling and beguiling to plainly despotic and threatening: "So, it's a deal. Tomorrow. Not another word. Now let's go back there."

I wanted to respond, but couldn't. He had subdued me completely. Cunningly, without my own will playing any part in it, he had turned me into his accomplice. I felt like screaming and crying.

On our way to look for Imaginaria, I wondered how to reverse the blind flight of a pact I hadn't agreed to. Oh, if I could only know! The white silence, the gray silence, the stunned silence, the alert silence, the vertiginous silence that put down roots, quick roots that move through the air and spin around and tangle and knot themselves around you until you can't get free. I was becoming the little animal lost among the thickets, the butterfly in the net, the blind stone sinking into water, no escape. I needed to rise up and cry "No!" with the emphatic voice of the Old Testament.

"Hey, I don't know. I'll think about it. Probably not!" I said forcefully in a sudden outburst, trying to pull my hand away from Juan's sweaty hand, but he only squeezed my fragile bones harder.

"Pshh! Hush. Tomorrow. It's all decided. I'm in charge here," he asserted sharply, in a low voice.

By now we had gotten to the place where Imaginaria was seated on a chest between two gypsy women. On the floor was the bundle she'd been carrying. But no one had a flame in her hand. One of the gypsies, the older one, was carefully studying one of Imaginaria's hands, as if looking for something, while she smoked energetically. The other was using a toothpick to stir a broken egg that was slipping off the plate. In spite of my distress, I remember taking note of these and other details. Both of them had long blue braids, blue moles—even their skin seemed to exude a blue hue. In their clothes, which appeared to be cut from a many-colored field, the prominent color was of course solferino.

"Here is the man that will leave you, the one with the stab wound," said the older one, showing her filthy teeth between puffs of smoke.

"Here is your misfortune, your black luck, about to appear," said the younger.

"And here is the girl who's coming to look for her, the morning star," said Juan, cutting off the last word. "Meet Laila and Vera." He pushed me forward and then left.

All three of them had spoken almost in a singing voice, but also in a tone of warning that wavered between promise and threat.

I wanted to get out of there. It all seemed dangerous to me: the place, the gestures, the voices. I felt that everything could start to take on the disquieting, inevitable hue of solferino.

Imaginaria was staring wild-eyed. She stared at her hand, at the plate, at me.

"Where? Where are they?" she stammered at last, her excitement at a pitch, as if the man, the misfortune, and I all belonged to a world that was being pulled away from her, and we needed to step forward and shout "Present!" to make ourselves visible.

"In your hand. The man is at this crossroads," clarified Laila, the gypsy with the broken yellow teeth, with a smile that was meant to be soothing.

"In the egg, don't you see? The misfortune is this tangle of hairs inside the egg," countered Vera, her eyelids sleepy but her gaze like lightning, using the toothpick to stir that messy and disgusting mixture in whose center a blackish thing is shining.

"And I am here, and we have to go now, right now, because they're waiting for us," I urge her desperately, touching her arm. She keeps looking at her hand and the plate, unconvinced.

"Yes, yes, the misfortune, the man, Lía—I can see them. Where are my twenty pesos?" she finally asks.

"Ah! You want your twenty pesos too? Your twenty pesos are gone. You have to pay if you want them to show you," explains Vera with measured exasperation. She brings her face up close, but stares into the distance.

"Pay who? To show me what? You told me you'd give them back," answers Imaginaria, suddenly realizing and on the verge of tears.

There is a sound like a sinister cackle. The old one lets out a quick, hoarse guffaw wrapped in smoke. Vera shrugs her shoulders and recites in a monotone: "You have to pay them, the ones over there," and she points with her ring-laden hand in the direction of the church tower—or could it be our dovecote? "They showed you the misfortune, didn't they? They showed you the man, didn't they? You saw them, didn't you? Do you think I kept your money, darling? I put it with the egg, just to see, and they took it and pulled all this rubbish out of you—don't you see, honey?"—all of this. And she goes back to stirring the toothpick in the nauseating substance that slides around the plate and even seems to be looking at me, although she doesn't even notice it. Could there really be an eye? And hair? Or is it just a couple of turkey feathers?

The older one turns toward the other and reprimands her in a low, dry tone, in a strange language. It's clear she doesn't reproach her for not returning the money, but for giving excuses, since every time she looks at Imaginaria she seems ready to fall on her and to erase her from sight with a slap of her hand and a click of her tongue. Vera's replies are quick, cross, and shrill, in contrast to her fixed expression. Theirs is a frenetic counterpoint, a quick, raucous, hissing, hacking duel, an unbearable vibration of lightning-fast serpents' tongues.

"Let's go, Imaginaria," I say as loudly as I dare. "They aren't going to give it back to you."

The duel comes to a quick halt, as if a referee had intervened.

"Go on, go with her, Maquinaria, and stop crying," Laila is quick to offer, and immediately, addressing me with the most shameless fawning: "You understand, darling child. You are nervous, fussy and well-bred, but when you grow up you're going to make any man happy. I can tell by your forehead. You heard it from me, golden girl. Go with God, both of you, and with the Virgin and the Archangel Michael…"

Imaginaria stands up, picks up her bundle, and takes me by the hand, and we start to leave without saying goodbye. I turn to make sure nobody is following us, and she moves her head backwards and forwards, to-and-fro, like a sullen chicken.

"…with the Archangel Gabriel, with the Angel Anael…," her voice continues, getting louder and louder.

When we get to the door, Juan the Alchemist isn't there. I'm not sure which angel guided us to that point, but undoubtedly he's the one who heard Imaginaria, who turned and shouted as she opened the door, "Thieves! Now I know who stole the turkeys! Turkey thieves!"

And without waiting we ran across the dusty street.

After the first moment of relief, I began to feel a gnawing worry again. I had made up my mind not to carry out what I hadn't promised, of course, but I wondered what the consequences might be for my unforgivable escapade. There was a threat. What did it hide? Juan had probably told the others of his plan. I would have to go back to the camp, to send word, to provide some explanation. If I didn't, they could come and make their demand, denounce me in front of my parents. I needed help. I decided to tell Laura everything. She listened attentively. When I had finished, she said with unexpected calm:

"You won't go explain anything, and neither will I. But I'll fix things. Nothing has been signed. You didn't even accept. And besides, if you go back, they'll kidnap you. Let me handle it. You can go dig a hole to China." By which she meant I could forget about the matter. I tried, but I couldn't. I fell asleep very late, amongst doubts, sinister images, and moans.

I woke up with a sudden start. Someone else's hand was there next to mine, underneath the pillow. Who was there? What did they want? Stealthily I brought my hand close, clutched at the other, strange, foreign one, and gave it a pinch. It was my own left hand, which had gone numb. I looked at the clock: it was past seven. Laura, barefoot and in her nightgown, was peering out to the street through a crack in the blind.

I tried to get up but couldn't. I was tied to the bed by a rope that encircled my knees and my waist—as will happen over and over again for many years, each time the gypsies come to town.

That's when I always hear Laura's voice saying:

"I tied you up so you wouldn't go out and tell them anything. They're gone now. The danger's passed."

When I stand at the window, I can still see a half-hidden gleam wherever I look, a light the color of solferino, a Luciferian sun.

St. John's Day Bonfires

. . .

All afternoon the path between the storehouse and the street was an ant track, because all of us—Laura, Miguel, Ruth, Cristina, and sometimes Imaginaria—were carting logs, lathes, kindling, any kind of wood we could use for the bonfire without polluting the air, according to the strict rules Papa and Mama had established. Luis María was in charge of the operation, María de las Nieves gave instructions, and Nanni sawed boards and carried them, clutching them tight and zigzagging as if he were dancing.

Every time we passed Nanni, who with his tattered frock coat, bowler hat and white sneakers always seemed to spring out of some crazy illustration, he would greet us by tipping his hat, revealing his drenched hair childishly marked by the teeth of a comb.

"Good afternoon, Principinas," he would say with a solemn bow, "Good night, good day."

"Goodbye, goodbye, goodbye," Laura and I would answer, respecting his fondness for threes.

When María de las Nieves joined us to help push the wheelbarrow, she dared to ask him: "Why don't you take off your hat and leave it on the rack, Nanni dear? It'll save you some work."

"And how am I going to greet you over here, if my hat is over there?" he asked, baffled by her display of ignorance.

"Well, if you have to say hello, say it without the hat," answered María de las Nieves, quickly dismissing this difficult problem.

"Oh, no, no, no, Eldest Princess! Greeting others without a hat is molto pitiful, wretched, disgraceful," Nanni ruled, offended to the core, and went on his way.

As evening fell the horizon slowly began to catch fire. The flames spread as the shadows were falling, and a cloud of smoke with its sad scent reached down the broad streets like a soul fleeing from hell. And into hell they seemed to be hastening, those figures in the distance that were jumping over the flames. It was a beautiful and disturbing spectacle, one that caused a keen sense of melancholy, as if at the very moment it was witnessed, it turned into a memory, entering into The Land of the Lost.

Now we had taken our places around the bonfire: Laura, Miguel, María de las Nieves, Luis María, Ruth, Cristina, Imaginaria, Nanni, and three or four more kids from the neighborhood who, dazzled by the blaze, had come to join our circle. It had been easy to pull us together because we had all been waiting impatiently for the fire to ignite and flare up so we could begin the ceremony.

And so we began, our hearts beating hard as in a ritual. Our faces shone, enraptured, while we moved around in a circle holding hands, arms crossed like scissors that open, scissors that close, to the beat of the chant and the dance:

Aserrín, aserrán,
(although maybe it said *Hacen rin, hacen ran,* imitating the sound of the saw)
los maderos de San Juan
piden pan, no les dan;
piden queso, les dan un hueso
*y les cortan el pescuezo.**

With a modest touch of good will, I changed the lyrics, singing softly so no one could hear:

* See note on page 167.

pide pan, se lo dan;
pide queso, le dan un beso
y le acortan el almuerzo.

Round and round again. Each time, with a beat that grew faster and faster, wilder and wilder. Our faces glowed, becoming more and more distorted and blurred in that shining, dizzy, bedeviled circle, that spinning wheel.

Suddenly it stopped. I was reeling like a drunk. Now you had to jump over the fire and make a silent wish, which God would grant to you. Just one wish—there wasn't time for more, like when a shooting star streaks across the heavens, perhaps writing wishes in the sky with the luminous twinkling that could be its secret code. Maybe the flames write them too, and send them skyward with the smoke, like the star with its light, so that they can fulfill their destinies. Light and fire: two emissaries that can foretell and transmit thought.

Imaginaria hasn't singed her hair, as she was afraid she would, and María de las Nieves leapt spectacularly—"like in the circus," "like in the Olympics," everybody keeps saying. Luis María knocked a log off the pile, but he argues that he meant to, that he did it with utter mastery. Miguel got a round of applause since he jumped with a pole like a perfect champion. I don't know how Ruth managed to jump—I didn't watch her. I've been somewhere else, thinking about how to do it, not only because I could never jump that high, but because I have the basilisk in my pocket, an egg laid by a rooster which for some odd reason I picked out of a clutch of hens, and which if it breaks will let the basilisk escape. If the basilisk looks at me, it'll turn me into stone or something even worse. Me or anyone it looks at. That's why I can't just leave it anywhere, because someone could break it by accident and be turned into marble or ruby or sapphire, which, no matter how precious, still signifies a difficult destiny. I've heard it said that if you put a mirror on your forehead so that the basilisk himself is the one he looks at, he dies of fright or of his own fulminating gaze. But who's to know he won't first look down lower? And besides, going around with a mirror stuck to your forehead isn't easy to explain, as if it had just happened by accident, as if you could say "I don't know! I didn't do it!" And meanwhile I'm missing the spectacle of this fleeting purgatory we're rehearsing. Cristina has jumped over one side of the fire, where the flames are lower and less ferocious. And Laura's done the same. Both of them were booed, but they applaud each other.

And now it's my turn. What should I do? And how? I hesitate, facing the fire that's unapproachable and beguiling, and just at the moment when something, someone, my guardian angel, my other self, snatches me through the air, I glimpse opposite me the face of Miguel, engraved in incandescent red over all the dark, unknown, invisible corners of my future, and I make my fervent wish, though I don't know how I'm moving, nor toward what.

Toward the ground, toward the other side, where I fall on top of Nanni—my something, my someone, my guardian angel, who has carried me piggy-back in a prodigious flight, over the fire, through the purifying vapor, and now lies with the edge of a coattail, or maybe a wing, backstitched by a quick little flame.

"Safe and sound, little princess!" he exclaims with the voice of the ace of spades, while he buries that voracious sparkle in the sand. "Vincitori!" In Nanni Fittipaldi's mind, there is no Joan of Arc, no matter how much she might want to be.

Did he really believe that I was about to throw myself in the fire? Nothing could have been further from my intentions. This is so true that I've stopped playing the "traveling tree" game. What does that have to do with it, you ask? Everything has to do with everything, even if you barely scratch the surface of meaning. To play traveling tree, Laura climbs to the top of any tree. I stay on the ground and run quick circles around the tree holding onto the trunk, as if we were running circles around the world. Suddenly I stop: we've arrived at a port or a station, and I shout the name of some country or city, and then I say "What do you see?" She pretends to be seeing everything she names, until I start turning circles again, or she stops, and in that case she loses and I climb the tree, and we keep going. The fun part is when we name something we're not sure belongs to that place, or something that can't belong, or that can belong to any place at all, or all three together, as always. But I'm talking about when Laura gets bored and shouts "Game change!" and then she comes down from the tree, manages to tie me to the trunk, and then I'm Joan of Arc and she's all the others, the ones who interrogate and judge, and ever since the last time, when she said she was going to look for matches to light the bonfire and I made my escape; I haven't wanted to play that ever again. Of course I'm sure I wouldn't get burned, but if she likes to pretend I would, it's easy enough for me to pretend I'm afraid.

Afraid, did I say? What could have happened in the meantime with the basilisk? Oh I hope the egg hasn't broken and isn't going around turning people to stone! No—the first one would be me, and I can still open one eye and then the other, or bring things close or move them away as I please, and miraculously the egg is intact in my pocket. I'm going to throw it into the fire.

By this time the flames have died down a little. A floor of coals is forming beneath a structure of burning gold, out of which blue goblins flee from menacing red-hooded sentries. On the periphery a strip of ashes, a border of half-charred logs marks the somber boundary of a territory no one should enter. Except the basilisk, of course, which needs to be destroyed. I take it carefully out of my pocket and fling it into its hell. The ones there seem to have taken it right in. But nothing noticeable has changed. There's just a slight curling of some of the sentries to indicate that it's being annihilated. And no, not a single sinister shape, no perverse soul comes twisting and swelling out of the basilisk's last breaths. Only a little last flickering, a tiny tremble, and it's over.

No one has realized what happened. Everyone is sitting on the ground, motionless, staring fixedly at the fire, except for Ruth, who's looking at Miguel as if hypnotized by his face and not by the shapes in the flames like all the others. The eyes glow in faces reddened like lamps. Maybe the "redskins" have that name because they're always lit up, sitting around a fire, smoking a pipe or sending smoke signals here and there. Maybe if we had a St. John's bonfire every day, we would be redskins too.

In the distance certain fires rage up brilliantly, while others shrink down and flicker out. The sky, always so blue and so close, takes on a vague lilac hue, the shade of a damp poplar tree. This must be the color of wakefulness, of insomnia, of those who stand watch. Because this night is not completely dazzling and joyful, like Christmas Eve, for instance. Maybe it's because of the cold of June, maybe because of the scent of goodbye and weeping contained in the clouds of smoke, which seem to be exhaled by time that is burning—and not only by time burning in this moment, but by what will come later, already marked, already eaten away by the anticipation of memory.

And just then, when Imaginaria and Luis María come carrying more firewood, María de las Nieves warns us:

"Time's up. This is the last round. Everybody in their place. The older ones are going to play with the grownups. The younger ones will do as they're told. Let's go!" And she claps hard three times, with that authority they have delegated to her, no doubt to force her into obedience.

Three handclaps, and we're dancing and singing. I don't like having fun under anyone's orders. But what's good about this ring, this wheel, is that I can circle around holding Miguel's hand, now without fear of the basilisk or worry about jumping, although on Miguel's other side is Ruth, writhing about like a blonde centipede. And here we go, our arms to one side and then to the other, while we jump and repeat:

Hacen rin, hacen ran,
los maderos de San Juan;
pide pan, se lo dan;
pide queso, le dan un beso,
y le apartan el escuerzo.

Which is Miguel's true hand? The left one, in Ruth's whitish and doughy hand? Or this other one that squeezes my hand that's like a throbbing bird, like a lone leaf that quivers? And could this be my own hand trembling, or Miguel pressing it? Couldn't it also be a message like that of smoke signals or stars, which I don't know how to decipher? And doesn't it pass from one to the other, all around the circle? It occurs to me that I've kept making my wish silently and that maybe it has collided with someone else's, someone who is making the same wish. Wishes that find each other? Not opposites, but opposed to each other because they're exactly the same.

Aserrín, aserrán,
hacen rin, hacen ran,
los maderos de San Juan.

There! It broke off, it's suddenly over. We stopped all at once and let each other go. I was left fluttering inside of myself, helpless, unfastened from everything, from the hand, from the secret current that held me up. I was still falling, facing the fire, rapt, entranced, when Laura and Cristina came up.

"Lía, where are you? Let's go inside. Let's go play something else," they insisted.

I walked away looking back at the remains of the bonfire.

When we tried to go into the living room, they didn't let us in. María de las Nieves and Luis María had taken their place among the grownups, who were playing the San Juan dare game. I knew how it went. In one bag they would put little pieces of paper with the names of the men, and in another the names of the women. Someone would take one piece of paper out of each bag, and before reading the names, would give the pair a task. They said that one of the most dangerous ones was having to kiss simultaneously, from opposite sides, a pocket watch that someone would suspend between the two players. If the person holding it yanked the watch away suddenly, just at the right moment, the pair could be stuck together forever. But forever and ever?

Miguel stayed out in the yard, hiding behind a palm tree, spying on the activities in the living room. He would tell us about it later. Laura, Cristina, Ruth, and I were like errant little gusts of wind that didn't know what cracks to filter through. After wandering through several places as if we were moving through different pictures ("Old Ladies Sipping Tea Made of Nasty Herbs," "Fathers Playing Cards," "Mothers Whispering," "Hallway Visited Only by Cold and Smoke"), we settled into our room as we'd been told.

"What were you singing?" asked Ruth absently, looking at me in the mirror while she tried to fix her unkempt hair.

"What for? Since when? How far?" I said, imitating Laura's way of answering with three silly questions that disarmed any curiosity.

"That's exactly what I say," Laura intervened mockingly. "And why are you so interested in everything Lía says or does?"

"Because she always does or says things differently from everybody else, secret things. Isn't that right?" answered Ruth, smiling like a guardian witch.

"If they're secret, then don't expect her to tell you," Laura finished victoriously.

"Speaking of secrets, why don't we play something?" ventured Cristina, and by speaking of secrets, she proposed, with a subtle sense of the opportunity involved, that we each write down what we had silently wished for when we jumped over the bonfire. Then we would fold the pieces of paper and collect them, and someone would read them aloud and we would all try to guess what everyone's wish was, writing our guesses down and not saying them aloud. Finally we would see the answers and the one who had guessed the worst would pay the penalty.

"Yes, yes!" shouted Ruth, so excited that it was as if heaven were already granting her plea. Laura didn't agree to this, but neither did she disagree, and Cristina began right away passing out pencils and pages she tore out of a little notebook.

I thought the game was silly. If I had shouted "Make Miguel love me!" as I passed over the flames, why should I have to write it now so that Laura, Cristina, and Ruth herself would know? Wasn't the wish granted only if it was kept secret? No, I couldn't write that down. I couldn't lie either. Actually, I hadn't jumped, if you mean "jumped" by my own devices. I could make this argument, but not only would it be obvious here that I was trying to find a way out, but there my wish wouldn't count for anything either. I looked at Laura in desperation. I saw that she was glancing at me sideways and shaking her head a little. She was saying no, I knew, but I didn't understand to what. Then suddenly I got it, as if a luminous wing had lightly grazed my forehead. The M, just the M, just the initial. Wasn't it acceptable to use initials even on handkerchiefs? Laboriously I wrote Make M. love me.

"Give them to me," ordered Laura.

And that's how we did it. As she got each one, she would crease it once more and put it in her pocket. Then she mixed them up slowly. She took one out. She held it high in her fist.

There was a moment of paralyzing expectation. My breath was escaping from me behind the pendulum of my heart.

Laura lowered her hand slowly, measuring time with the clock of eternity, unfolded the paper, read it, passed her gaze over each one of us, and recited as if from a pulpit: "I want them to give me a pony and a bicycle and make the ants die."

Those were three things, not one. But I wasn't going to protest. Let them protest there. Anyway, everyone knew that a pony and a bicycle sped through Cristina's dreams, hoping to reach her moment of awakening. If she was now adding a cemetery of ants, fine—that would make the garden happy. I wrote neatly on my piece of paper: 1. Cristina.

Laura repeated the suspense. Now she was looking at the second wish. She said placidly: "May it rain in Guatraché, in Catriló, and in Gamay while I dance in the Colón Theater." It had to be Laura. She wanted to learn dances, and she had heard—as I had—that our fields were threatened by drought. She was so clever that she had managed to fold several wishes into one. While she whirled round and round inside the rectangle of light on a stage, rain would resound like a glass instrument accompanying the orchestra from remote plantations. I hoped that by that time they wouldn't already be wastelands. I noted tenderly: 2. Laura.

Only Ruth and I were left. The confession that Laura was about to read at that moment belonged to one of us.

"Blank paper," she said in a neutral tone, her expression indifferent.

"Blank paper? That's the wish? How weird!" Cristina and I complained in turn, incredulously.

"No, dummies. Somebody didn't write anything. The paper is blank—" and she showed us both sides.

Ruth was looking at us with her neck very stiff and an asp's smile that looked like the groove of a screw.

I felt the fury of a fiery lash across my face. Cheater! Traitor! And I had been so scrupulous as to write the initial. I felt my good faith was being mocked, along with my honor and my conduct for the entire future. There were shadows lying in ambush in the entryways, insects that scurried swiftly behind doors, floors that were being pulled out from under my feet. And beyond all this deceit, my immolation was still imminent, betrayed by my own handwriting, to mock and humiliate me. It was inevitable. I was about to run away crying when I heard, in Laura's firm and triumphant voice:

"Blank paper. Another blank paper. And that's it." And she waved it over her head like a trophy, between her agile fingers.

That was impossible. Where was my confession? And where did that answer come from?

"That can't be, it can't be"—Ruth jumped up and moved toward Laura, shaking her head "No" furiously with both arms in the air.

"And why can't it be?" asked Laura serenely. "Or maybe you're the only one who knows how to be clever?"

"It can't be, because that paper had to have been Lía's, and if it was hers, she wouldn't have been so surprised to see another blank paper," she confirmed with the infallible certainty of a theorem.

"And why did it have to be Lía's? It could be or not be. And couldn't she have faked being surprised? Or why couldn't she have wanted to dance the rain dance in the Colón Theater, and even have a pony and bury ants?" Laura's voice sounded firm, calm, with a certain touch of mockery and challenge, while she stuffed the last piece of paper with the others in her pocket.

"No, no, and no!" howled Ruth, stomping on the floor. "Let me see what you have in your pocket"—and she threw herself on Laura.

A violent struggle began between the two of them, in which Laura, in spite of her giggles, was at a disadvantage because she was younger and more fragile. Cristina and I were just about to jump in when Miguel showed up.

The fight was over. The explanations were over too. Laura casually emptied out her pockets. She began unfolding the pieces of paper: two with writing on them (Cristina's and her own) and two blank (Ruth's, and mine? erased by the angels?). The evidence was irrefutable, but nobody paid attention to the vote. Why should they?

The evening was over.

As they left, we followed everyone out to the front gate. As we watched them walking away, I asked Laura how she had done it.

"When your piece of paper came up," she told me, "I repeated mine from memory, I hid yours in my shoe and I put the one I was supposed to vote with in my pocket. I hadn't written anything on that one."

"And why did you do it?" I inquired, maybe gratefully, maybe as a reprimand, maybe in shame.

"What did you want me to do? Help you to tell your secrets so they could laugh at you? Were they really going to think that M stood for Mama, Methuselah, or Mancunario?"

"And who is Mancunario?" I exclaimed, flustered.

"Ah! Blank piece of paper."

I breathed in the pungent night air. The smell of a memory that returns, that has not yet burned itself out. Of course not: there in front of me were the last remnants of the fire, and through the glow, perforating both distance and time, the fatal gaze of Ruth, the gaze of the basilisk.

Written With Smoke

. . .

The first time I can't say there was any warning, unless you want to count the insistent, almost manic prolixity with which I cut out the pictures from the discarded *Gardening Manual* and pasted them onto the illustrations in *History of Argentina,* so that the first triumvirate was made up of a tulip, a carnation and a gardenia worn by the bodies of Chiclana, Sarratea and Paso. Don Narciso Laprida was decorated with the image that matched his name and the delegates to the Tucumán Congress became a handsome nursery overflowing with primroses and pansies waving their arms on high. But I can't be sure, without pushing the interpretation too far, that all this proliferation of color against a patriotic pantheon would have predicted the bouquets with which someone threatened us on Friday the 25th of May. They were three bouquets of roses, so faded that they were almost colorless. They showed up in the morning tied to the garden fence, totally ugly, dried up and sad. No one doubted that they were the embodiment of ill wishes, transmitters of harm, emissaries of misfortune.

The second time was the following Friday, and I felt it coming from the moment I saw the dried flowers. Day after day the unbearable closed-in feeling, even out in the fresh air, as if the interplay with the outdoor world—all that giving out blackness and bracken poison in nocturnal hibernation and receiving in exchange a washing of light—were at the verge of brusquely coming to a halt. No more even rhythm of breath in and out; they're lowering the lid now. And as if that weren't enough, the threat of increasing cold, rigidity and consumption that spreads from skin to bones and turns me into a bird with barely beating wings and lackluster feathers. That's what I've almost become, until a blind impulse, that later turned out to have been inspired, led me on Thursday to open all the birdcage doors. Nothing happened, except for the flapping of wings and skirts and the punishment that included isolation, dim light, and hunger. But the next day an unfamiliar person delivered the box, without including any message. There it was, open on the dining room table, exposing its dismal contents: a dead canary, choked to death, inexplicable, stirring up as many fears as conjectures.

During the whole following week I saw the blotch. Every night just as I was falling asleep, when this place loosens its mooring ties and begins to drift toward other places, or begins to become so porous, so permeable, that furniture, visitors and vivid pictures that were never here and wouldn't even fit start turning up, then the blotch would appear, tipping over images, and cut off the whole game with a good shake. It was a red, almost circular blotch, about the size of the moon. It would suddenly project onto the wall making me jump violently and cry out all at once. There it would be for a few instants and then disappear, no doubt chased off by my voice. While it was there, I felt as though it was watching me and that its expression was focused and evil. And Friday morning, after Pepa's shouts and reactions awakened the house, I managed to disobey the rules and slip out the garden door and walk all the way around, and I saw it exactly the same, brilliant and perverse, spilled over the threshold: a bloody warning, a premonition in whose dangerous reflections the grownups read a political message and Papa's sharp eyes must have deciphered certain names.

Did I sense the warnings? Did I record them in a register deposited in God's time? You could say I did. I don't know what for, given that they didn't lead to anything (or maybe they did; perhaps they made up the antecedents of a hidden sorrow, of an evil that became evident only much later on, of a misfortune that was assumed to be recent). But on the other hand, what could I have done to stave off the fulfillment of a tragic prediction or to counteract the effects of a fatality that surpassed all my possibilities? In any case those occurrences marked the beginning of surprising perceptions that, while they may not have taken place regularly, did present themselves with some frequency over the course of several years.

I can remember the episode that submerged me fully and unmistakably in that type of experience. I was in the deepest heart of Africa taming lions—sorry, but the singularity of the event would justify even this beginning. It was during an interminable summer afternoon siesta. Alone in my room, with the blinds closed, I could track, on the ceiling and on the walls, as in a camera obscura, the rapid movement of shadows projected from the street—one of my favorite spectacles, filled with unidentifiable images—when a totally different scene imposed itself over the rest. Only it did not come from outside. It was in me, like a memory, like an imaginary image, without being either the one or the other, but rather a concrete vision, sometimes hazy, sometimes sharp, similar to a photograph behind glass within the eye. From the beginning I felt that "that thing" did not have a calming quality and I tried to make it disappear, but I only managed to stir it up. It remained there stubbornly, despite my blinking, until I closed my eyes and it installed itself definitively. I accepted its tyranny with curiosity and apprehension. I saw that at that moment—extracted out of where? when?—it was night and that something profoundly menacing was over by the tree, even before I could make out the black horses that pulled up there and the dark, luxurious carriage. There was a break in the storm, a door opening, a lantern being extinguished. Something moved in the coachman's seat, someone jumped down, straightened up and showed his face. A very tall man with long coattails loomed up, in a top hat, with starched collar and cuffs, and gloves so white that they gleamed in the dusk. His long pale face looked a bit like a horse's, and the teeth revealed by his smile also looked a bit like a horse's as he displayed them, showing off his bristling and almost incandescent mane which had to be false. He spun around, still holding his top hat high, as he helped two blurry figures down from the upper seat. They were slow and awkward, short in height, all hair and layers of clothing, that once on the ground turned out to be Laura and me, both of us dressed as angels. They moved forward, or we moved forward, hesitantly, perhaps reluctantly, perhaps against all of History. In my mind a low, twangy voice, very solemn, almost sang a reproach: "You're forgetting the flowers." We continued on without stopping, without looking backward, presumably toward the door, and suddenly it all disappeared. Without losing time I got out of bed, ran barefoot out of my room, crossed the hall, and rushed into the living room to see us enter. There was no one there. Through the panes of a window I could see the bushes across the way, the single tree, the street empty in the golden light.

What had all that meant? What could a coach like that be doing in front of our house at any hour of day or night? And why were Laura and I traveling in it, dressed up as angels? Were we dead? Who was the strange and ceremonious gentleman who looked like a horse? A coachman from heaven? And who forgot the flowers? Whose was the voice that complained?

For days and weeks I tried out various stories, adding all kinds of elements to the ones I'd seen. The chain of events was always implausible, totally unbelievable, full of gaps and random bizarre juxtapositions. But the versions I tried out most often were those of the suspense-novel kidnapper and his two victims being returned home with the appropriate outfits and the flowers (Couldn't the voice have said, "They're forgetting the flowers?") and that of the scenario of the fortunate impresario and his stars in a chance break between wildly successful tours (Why were the three traveling on the coachman's seat?). Nor could the possibility of a carnival adventure be discarded, a deliberate party for a birthday or Christmas celebration, or even some fantastic episode connected with the beatification of a living person or the return of the selfsame guardian angel following a mysterious abandonment. I oscillated between naïveté and truculence, and between vanity and terror, in so many degrees and directions that I exhausted the fantasy and left it blank. In this empty framework, the coachman and the two girls with horses, coach and indecipherable night all slowly faded out and if they ever tried to return, their effort was like melted snow trying to reconstitute itself as snowflakes, or that of a dispersed cloud trying to collect itself again. I forgot about it.

The eighth of December was a dazzling but exhausting day. The procession left the church, took two turns around the plaza, then turned to go down the long road decorated with streamers and banners, and came out at the church on the other end. I walked along behind the float of the Virgin with my golden basket, tossing flowers every few steps all along the route. Even if the crown of flowers wasn't exactly too tight across my forehead, it irritated me, and it irritated me even more knowing that after taking it off, I'd keep feeling as though it was still there for several hours. Even now, don't I still occasionally feel something that's like a ghost of that crown, an oppressive nonexistent band around my head that I call the "little angel feeling"? Along with that little headpiece, the little fringe that brushes coldly against my face, and the singed wing fastened to the middle of my back constitute leftover traces or souvenirs of earlier lives, let's put it that way, since they've always been there without being there.

The solemnity of the procession, the hymns and the prayers, didn't give me a chance to turn around to look at Laura who was moving along in the same way, two angels back; even less could I bend over to clean out the grit and pebbles that got into my sandals and were hurting my feet. Stoically, I put up with the torture by trying not to limp, setting myself a series of little goals for stoicism, sniffing and holding back my tears like Moses and Joan of Arc. I could see the church in the distance, I could see it shimmer and distance itself with the cruelty of ever-unreachable beauty.

Once inside, after another ceremony that I attended barefoot, the gathering dispersed. I went over to Laura. We both had bleeding feet and we washed them under a faucet in the patio of the parish house. Our wounds weren't deep, but they turned the floor into a field of hard thorns and sharp-edged stones with every step. We looked for Natalina, who was supposed to be taking us home. It was hard for us to recognize her without her everyday apron, dressed almost like a Hungarian peasant, with lots of ribbons and embroideries and with her black hair loose as a curtain nearly drawn closed over her face. She was right there, in the crowd, standing under an acacia tree, looking as though she were asleep with her eyes open and wearing a blissful smile as if she were contemplating a sea of rainbow bubbles or a cherubim choir.

As we moved over toward her we entered the present: the immediate, the moment of now, of tomorrow.

"Is she there or isn't she?" whispered Laura, trying to catch Natalina's eye.

"She's still receiving the benediction," I answered her. I can find mystical explanations for any absence as well as for any supernumerary presence.

"Natalina, where are you? Come down: we need you. Come quickly, please," Laura insists, almost shouting, and tugging on one of her arms.

The descent is abrupt, as sudden as if a ladder had been pulled out from under her. Her startled face emerges between burst bubbles and scattered cherubim.

"Let's go, let's go, all right," she says automatically, gesturing in the air.

"We can't walk," explains Laura. "Our feet are injured, full of cuts, nicks, scrapes, wounds, sores, and gashes." Her voice gets sadder and sadder as she exaggerates more. She's trying to make us cry.

"All right, never mind, I can't walk, either," answers Natalina, showing us the very high heels of her red shoes. "I'm going to have to have them cut down. That would be better, much better," she adds with that optimism that makes her invincible, even in the worst situations. "Let's go outside and get a ride home in a car."

We headed for the back door, the three of us limping along painfully, she leaning forward from time to time as if she were on skates leading the charge, and the two of us moving along so cautiously it was as if we were trying to sneak up on someone.

There's no one in the street. Everyone must be in front of the church, or in the plaza or at the festival being held at the club. We sit on the bench on the sidewalk to wait for whoever's car, it doesn't matter whose, as long as it comes, but we don't even have time to take off our sandals when we hear a very solemn voice behind us.

"Here I am. Rafael Orfani, for whatever the delightful young ladies would like to request."

I turn around, struck by the lightning bolt. It's obvious that he's there. The very tall, impeccably dressed man is not unfamiliar. He sweeps off his hat and reveals bristly hair that tops his horsey face, while he smiles disclosing enormous teeth. I follow him with my gaze, incredulous and no doubt terrified, as he moves around the bench, until he bends over in front of Natalina and extends a gloved hand:

"We can depart whenever the little lady wishes. That's how I am. The car is just around the corner. It seemed like a good idea, you know.

Although there is nothing to fear, there is nothing to worry about." The long-jawed face tries out some expressions to illustrate reassurance.

Natalina stands up, struggles to get to her feet leaning on the bent arm of the gentleman and partly submerged again in the cloud of bubbles and cherubim. Laura and I follow them as best we can, almost lurching along, fully concentrated on moving forward. Despite this I manage to hear:

"An escort of angels, just what you deserve, rosebud. If you weren't walking along, you'd look like a flower. Lean on me, that's it. Here I am, straightforward, strong, and diligent, at your service, ladies."

Natalina's nervous laugh indicates that if it's for her talent for walking, she might well win the contest for queen of the flowers. But I can't quite figure out what role I'd play in that scheme, and now we've all turned the corner and I can't believe what I'm seeing. Standing there is a huge funeral coach, immense, shiny, coal black, drawn by two horses with black plumes, and the pair of them are headed toward it, and the one climbing up onto the driver's seat of the hearse, helped by the man, is our ineffable Natalina. I look at Laura asking for help. Her face is overflowing with silent laughter.

"We can't get into that. Please, let's not go in that," I beg with desperate urgency.

"Why not? It's got wheels, right? Or would we rather walk?"

No, we wouldn't rather walk. If I don't prefer to walk, I enter into this tyrannical or charitable plural that frees me from being all alone, stopped on the threshold, behind the glass, or on the other side of the ditch. I can install myself in it as in the common lair and share the cold, the apprehensiveness, and the pebble soup. From there, I'll begin to multiply my participation indefinitely until I'm totally integrated, until I can switch places with anyone, dissolving myself in a unit that is vaster than the universe. "Let me in, make room for me," I'll clamor over and over again in silence from my isolation, from my insufficiency, while they slam the door in my face or the circle closes, leaving me outside it, where I am left alone, twisting and braiding the strands of my pale garland.

"Make room for me," I shout from the air, through which I'm moving fast in the man's arms, blessed and abominable arms that deposit me on Natalina's lap.

We squeeze together as best we can, the four of us on the high driver's bench, decorated with carvings, wings and pleats, and the coach starts rolling with slow vehemence, while the three of us take off our shoes and Rafael says we'll go for a ride through the neighborhood, distributing splendor and joy.

"I'd have liked to be able to offer you the mourners' coach," he explains. "It's much more comfortable, but here we all ride together, very close together, right, precious? Tell me the truth, have you ever ridden in a coach like this?"

"Like this one? No, I don't think so. No, definitely not. This one is much better," Natalina reacts gradually, and ends with certainty: "This is a nice coach. Unique."

"Unique, yes. That's the word for it, sweetheart. I'm unique, I'm like a diplomat, an introducer of ambassadors."

We move along ceremoniously, on exhibit. It's as though we're traveling on a scaffold, on a ladder, or in a walnut tree, but only because of the height. Because the sensation is that of floating along freely in an articulated and buoyant wooden organism, in a kind of antediluvian monster created in the carpentry shops of Lethe. It rocks, creaks, oscillates and sways its squalid fleshless haunches. It dodges along, its rigid ribs lurching. The fragile bones of the steeds of death will fall apart. We're all going to be hurled into a ridiculous heap at the side of the road. Let's hope. Let's hope no one is watching this humiliating, macabre and carnivalesque journey. I'm dying of shame, of nausea, of repressed exasperation. Well, I would be dying, if the place weren't so ridiculously redundant. Isn't it awful enough to be where I am?

I look over at Laura: she's happy, she's doing something new, she's alive, transforming a vehicle of the dead. She's a pioneer of the desert pampa, just like Papa. I look at Natalina: not only is she not complaining about anything, but she's feeling as though she's on a throne way up in the sky. She's enthralled by contemplation of her miracle, sure to be "the best." I look at Rafael, full of pride in his role as funerary coach driver, dispenser of the most exquisite care and of the most delicate posthumous tributes. He hasn't stopped talking since we started driving. He has compared his function with that of a diplomat charged with maintaining good relations between two apparently hostile territories, and with that of a pilot transporting a passenger to the most secure port ("And aren't we all passengers, my dear? Ah, no, don't fear that I'll leave you! With respect to you, I'll be like a clinging vine, sweet dove."); he has spoken with enthusiasm of the dark horses with a funereal vocation that have come galloping from Orlof. He has said that this coach is to the plains what the gondola is to Venice! ("Haven't you seen how it rocks us, beloved? And both of them are black, too, coal black like the fire in your eyes, dear heart.") because besides this, the dead may well be the lovers of death and that's why they don't return ("Ah, don't look at me that way, dear treasure, because it kills me! But dead and embalmed, I'd return for your kiss.") and sweet songs should be sung to them while driving along, songs like the gondoliers sing, as they row couples out to gaze at the ghostly moon over the canals. That gives him the opportunity to sing several Italian canzonette in a fervent tone wearing an expression of horsey agony, while Natalina accompanies him leaning her head on his shoulder and humming between sighs, and Laura fills in the pauses calling out, with souls in purgatory, "Break, break my chains! Give me freedom!"

They're all so pleased with themselves that when two or three kingfishers fly up out of the road terrified, and two men picking fruit in the top of a tree freeze in place, hanging from the branches, and a group of boys who look as though they're dressed up as beetles wearing baskets stop playing their game and stare at us open mouthed, and an old beggar woman plasters herself against a wall with her tattered feathers rumpled and crosses herself, my companions smile at each other with profound contentment, as if each of these reactions had been the true and single purpose of so much rowdiness. I'm sure they're sorry they don't have any confetti or streamers with which to leave a festive trail along our route.

And now we've completed the spectacular demonstration by stopping in front of a shop from which Rafael has brought a jar of sangría, two orange sodas, four glasses, and three packets of cookies, as well as a bunch of curious onlookers who appear and disappear noisily and constantly, accompanying all their entrances and exits with shoves and laughs. All I do is swallow, as best I can, the ground glass of humiliation, and feel the bitter and intolerable taste of ignominy.

Now Rafael has gone over a wire fence and into a field where daisies, marigolds, periwinkles grow, mixed with weeds and other wild plants. He spins, runs, floats, leans over flapping his coat tails—a gigantic tuxedoed horse romping in the Eden of his stable yard—and ecstatically picks an armful of flowers with which he leaps and flies toward us, and comes by us and past us, and lays the flowers in the place where "they" always travel in their long varnished boxes, under the canopy, while he says to Natalina with the sweetness of someone crunching a honeycomb in his strong jaws:

"They're for you, my queen."

And it seems to me that we've already started to move when I say it. They may not even have heard me with the horses grunting, the loud cracking of the machinery, the bumblebees and the tremors of the seduction, the victorious children's trumpets and the applause and taunting whistles of those who were still around. It doesn't matter. Even if they don't ask me anything, I repeat for myself, for yesterday, for no one, with the thin and sententious voice of the smoke of Delphos:

"She's forgetting the flowers. She's going to forget them."

When we got there it was nighttime. While we walked wearily toward home and I hear the solemn and twangy voice murmuring "You're forgetting the flowers," I look toward the window where I should be peering out, waiting for us. I know perfectly well that I'm not there, but what I don't yet know is why I didn't also see her in my earlier vision of the past. I still don't know that it was foresight, either. I don't know yet that she stayed to collect the flowers, and that she remained with him, the funerary gentleman who courted her, who was already married and the father of three children, following who knows what strange destiny. We never saw each other again. The coach turned up a few days later, abandoned, with two pairs of gilded sandals, left at the station of a distant and dusty town.

Candles for the Emissaries

. . .

Now I know that they represent others and that I have no way to know whom. They are their doubles, their emissaries or their spies, and I also don't know what purpose has brought them here, although they all came in the best of hands. I didn't ask anybody anything when they arrived, and now I limit myself to keeping an eye on them, leaving them locked up in the study, which is also the game room. When I go back in there the next time, there is always something that has changed; I couldn't say exactly what, but the position of a head or a hand, some disarray of clothing, or a contrived appearance of calmness shows that they've tried to restage the scene at the speed of light, with a hastiness that blocks any view of whatever there is under something that's now transformed, like when a lizard streaks across a wall we're just about to focus on. I don't dare peek at them beforehand through the keyhole, because that might be worse: I could meet up with another eye, with a needle poking through, with the Basilica of Luján or an unbearable vision. Because, besides, who could give me any guarantee that this isn't what they expect me to do so they can reveal their true natures? And isn't it possible that this fear is a forewarning of that robot performance I saw in Paris, in the middle of a silent and deserted night, on the Rue Vaugirard, when I stooped over to look through the irresistible keyhole of a green door? It may be just a greeting, a mechanical bow, a bending over of the bald couple's articulated bodies under the dim, bloody light, nothing more than a warning that they've known that I'm here—barely a second's flash in eternity—and then, immediately, total darkness.

These three are women—or rather, girls, just to pretend that I believe in the simulation—and they have scant, regular, and abundant hair, respectively. I call them Gervasia, Melania and Adelia, but who knows what their names are. I wanted to give them names ending in "–ia" because it seems to me that they open, expand and hide and reopen the way some flowers do, and they turned out to be names of ancient old maids who inhabit mansions in ruins where everything looks purple colored, so unnerving that the attics and the cellars get mixed up with each other, under layers of spider webs and shreds of moleskin.

Gervasia looks like Queen Guinevere. That same look of a bride abandoned on her wedding day, with her fancy white dress faded and her garlands of stones and pearls that have lost their glow; only the few locks of hair protruding from her headdress are bright and her wide blue eyes seem to gaze resentfully at the advance of all the clock hands in a distant and foggy country. Melania is younger, even paler and so long-suffering that she seems to have traversed leagues of rain and hardships to have come this far, nearly exhausted, to ask for help, after calling fruitlessly for her father—"Paaaapa"—with her dark rainy hair and that terrified expression of someone who raced out just as she was, fleeing a fire, a flood, or wolves. Adelia, on the other hand, faces up proudly to all proposals, malicious or not, addressed to her or others, and she proclaims her satisfaction with that triumphant air and those gauzes and silks and ribbons and dress-up laces with which they used to pamper her, from her delicate slippers to her shiny golden curls. She'd like to be the queen, the one who gives the orders with her mouth half open showing off four teeth, bending her arm to hold a scepter or lifting a knee to ascend the steps up to her throne. Only here there are no scepters or thrones and all she can do is squeak out a protest saying "Maaaama," when she is tipped over, or close her eyelids with that "click," that impersonal sound of cracking ice. The other two stare silently, almost mutely. Gervasia is like a foreigner who doesn't understand, and Melania like someone who hasn't gotten over a huge scare.

I don't talk to them, as I've seen others do, making up different voices to say whatever people want to hear, to swear by outrageous lies or reveal the secrets of others. Although I'm not sure that the dolls' voices are not really their own, that it isn't the dolls who decide to do it this way. I don't mistreat them, either, not only because it isn't true that they have no feelings, and not because I fear them, but because I don't take advantage even of silence or of the good will of objects. I'd rather keep to an indispensable relationship, one that consists of moving them around, in getting them out of the way, in imagining that we're in an anteroom, each one in her place, like four strangers. In any case, in this anteroom together we've undergone storms, illnesses, punishments, static landscapes and so many comings and goings that I was almost fond of them. Until yesterday.

Yesterday afternoon Aunt Adelaida took me out with her to pay calls and to leave some jars of marmalade at María Teo's house. It's that bright, thick marmalade that Grandma makes, the kind where the jam flows very slowly across the glass jar as if it were giving it an endless kiss out of the pure joy of its color. In this case the happiness of the jam doesn't change, but it's only marmalade of "payback of favors, let's hope that shameless nasty witch doesn't give us anything in return," because every treat María Teo sends us ends up in the trash can, without even the dogs being allowed to try a bite, not because it's poisoned but because for sure she has put some disgusting thing into it so we'll all disappear except for Papa, according to what I heard Mama say when I was under the table and she thought I was somewhere else. I wouldn't mind disappearing, as long as we could all disappear together, since that must mean we'd reappear somewhere else that would soon be the same place since each one of us would keep being the same, but for that to happen Papa would have to be part of it. I also understand that Grandma wants to return a tooth for a tooth in order not to offend María Teo, because who knows what she'd be capable of doing then, but who knows what else Grandma is intending, since I've seen her and heard her mumble unintelligible sentences while she stirs and waits for the jam to be ready. Maybe she's praying for it to come out right, or for it to come out wrong, but maybe she's adding invisible ingredients to the recipe word by word.

I don't like to pay calls because I'm very pale and before we enter a house they pinch my cheeks over and over to put some color into them so no one will think I'm sick and about to infect everyone, like someone pretending to have contagious blotches or spots. I can't stand that odious and irritating pinching, but then several people in my family have died, people I didn't know—except for my brother Alejandro whose face and color were like mine—and it seems that everyone remembers them, maybe sitting or standing like in a photo, very quiet and very pale, I suppose in the living room where each one will try to disappear little by little into the mists of the Venetian mirror, in those really sick waters that will distribute them like rigid yellow nosegays—pale tea roses grown old in the living room—tossed into all the canals from black gondolas with plumes.

Aunt Adelaida is also afraid of something contagious because she always, without taking off her glove, wraps a scrap of paper around her fingertip before she rings any doorbell. She must be scared of something more, now, because she has stopped and has made me stop suddenly in front of the unthinkable door, after looking in all directions flapping her arms so that even the most unattentive person would notice her. Immediately she grabs me by one arm and moves forward, dragging me along through that dim hallway that I imagined filled with a hot acid stench: the caged-up breath that announces the proximity of the wild animal. The dark mass splattered with yellow chrysanthemums suddenly looms at the end, in an interplay of door, glass and reflection as instantaneous as destiny. The face of lying down, with one swollen eyelid lower than the other, breaks into a dirty chestnut-colored smile that makes that narrow insect head atop a disproportionately wide and craggy body look even more repugnant.

"Mama sends you this jam," says Aunt Adelaida, holding out her hand from as far away as if there were a puddle between the two of them. "But I really came with regard to that matter I told you about," she adds indecisively, with a little conspiratorial laugh.

"Yes, yes, I've been waiting for you for days. Come in. In the meantime, the child can play with my niece," María Teo answers as if she'd just yawned, while Adelaida scurries toward the vestibule with me clinging to her hand and to her skirts, and I enter stumbling into the multicolored jaws of destiny, managing to evade the heavy hand and gnawed fingernails that come down toward my head. "Don't be so standoffish. This must be Lía, right? What do you like to play? Cora, Corina, Corazón!" she yells sleepily, turning slowly.

You could say that, summoned by with that voice calling to her almost painfully, Cora, Corina, Corazón would have to appear even if through the smoothest wall in that place jammed full of wicker and woven fabrics. But no. Someone who doubtlessly is she and who must have been lurking there, appears instantly at one of the two doors to the right of the summoner. It is a child with the face of a grownup, wrapped in so much clothing that her shape might seem to be that of a musical spinning top, or a cabbage fallen from a rainbow, if one didn't notice immediately that like the slipcovers, the pillows and the decorations, she is a product of industrious obedience to the tyranny of a manual of crochet instructions. Under the cap that sags down around her neck, her enormous dark serious eyes stare fixedly, with justified mistrust of María Teo's demands.

"This is Cora, my niece, and this is Lía, Miss Adelaida's niece. Cora has been sick and shouldn't run or get excited, but the two of you should make friends and stay here playing while I show her aunt some designs," María Teo explains flatly.

"I want to see designs and soldiers and flowers to embroider and the lake where there are herons and flamingos that stand on one leg," says Cora in a voice that is surprisingly high for its volume, monotonous and insistent.

"No, miss. You're going to play Twenty Questions or I Spy or Who Blinks First or something else with your little friend here until we come back," María Teo commands in the same sleepy tone, while she takes Aunt Adelaida by one arm and steers her in the direction of the other door on the right, that no doubt leads to the other room at the front of the house.

"I don't want to play anything with my little friend who has the face of a Chinese jellyfish; I don't want to, even if she wants to and even if everyone else begs me please until the end of time," the little wrapped package now articulated energetically and impersonally, as if she were repeating a grammar exercise, while she marked the beat with one foot, but only I heard the end, because the door banged shut immediately and I lost sight of the threat of printed yellow flowers and green pleats that protected me.

"What's a Chinese jellyfish?" I asked imprudently, undecided between offense and conciliation.

She inspects me with embarrassing fixedness. Her hard-candy eyes look me over in detail from my hair to the tips of my toes. I begin to suspect that she won't bother to answer me when she says:

"It's something from a storybook that you can't see in the water and you can see what's behind it even if it wants to hide, but it isn't glass or mica or gelatin or anything that shows up under any kind of light," she explained unhesitatingly, in one of her brilliant linguistic performances.

"Something transparent?" I ask, without wanting to say invisible because I suspect her of referring to my game of making myself invisible, but without knowing how she's managed to find this out, let alone finding out if I've ever succeeded.

"Something transparent is too little, rare, insufficient. It's not enough because something transparent is always visible if it is colored, like sapphire, garnet, emerald, a thermometer, a magnifying glass, grenadine or wine, and to see the Chinese jellyfish well you have to get it to drink Chinese tea and say the short words that I know, pointing your index finger at the sun," she says with ample erudition about transparencies, as if she'd spent her life submerging objects, with solid magical and syntactic expertise. Despite this I notice that there's an error in her reasoning, but I don't know how to refute it.

On the other hand, since I'm getting to like the idea of being a Chinese jellyfish, I ask anxiously:

"So are you going to give me Chinese tea and say the words?"

"No, because you already appeared, and I don't know how to get you to disappear again, and that's a good thing because otherwise they'd give me a good beating and take me over to Grandma Eduviges's house where they make me drink milk with cream and castor oil and cod-liver oil and all that disgusting stuff that smells of disinfectant and cockroaches that it's better to not talk about," and after this show of oratory, she adds with surprising brusqueness: "Is your Aunt Adelaida your mother?"

"No, at home Aunt Adelaida is my aunt, and Mama is my mother.

There's one of each category," I explain, embarrassed both by the simplicity of our customs and by the abundance they represent.

"Ah, because you have a really big house, with sheds and gardens! Here, my aunt is Mama, I think, because there isn't another one. But she doesn't want me to say this and if I do say it, she sends me over to Grandma Eduviges's house where I have to kiss the saints every little while and I spend the mornings up in the tree and the afternoons on top of the wardrobe because they look for you with a spoon in hand and even climb a ladder to get to you. Spoons are pretty boring, don't you think? But if they're empty and you look at them, you see yourself upside down, with your head pointed down. Do you like dolls?" she adds with sudden inspiration after the varied but connected speech.

"Not much. It depends on their faces," I say unenthusiastically, but I can already imagine the parade coming up: each participant with her little outfits (also crocheted) and their necklaces and their tea sets and their virtues and their defects and even their illnesses, which would no doubt be fearful and endless in the mouth of their chatty young owner. "There are three that live with me. The others are put away," as though that took care of the subject.

Not only did I not put an end to it, but even opened it up to the worst.

"I've got lots. All the ones I love and the ones I don't love, too. But she has them working for her, putting them to use every Friday. Still, I'm going to show them to you anyway, so you'll see. So you'll know. First we'll go listen, because they aren't looking at patterns: they are playing cards. And then I'll show them to you, because I want to, because I've thought of it, because I feel like it." I realize that she was talking about the dolls, and then about Aunt Adelaida and María Teo, and then about the dolls again.

She puts a finger to her lips and moves silently, gesturing me to follow her and pushing open the door through which she appeared when we arrived.

The room is dim, but there is a translucent screen that lets though an alarming reddish glow, as though there were a fire blazing in a corner. In the air there floats an odor of dense smoke, greasy smoke, smoke of a secret burning. It's strange: such a diffuse glow and such sadness. It makes one want to cry.

The door that opens onto the next room is half open, and through that crack of clarity, which isn't any more consoling, Aunt Adelaida and María Teo could be seen sitting facing each other across a table, settled there for years, until they get old. I don't like what we are doing. We stick to the wall without making any noise and we hear María Teo's voice, complaining and languid, as if she were struggling to open a passageway between sleeping islands, between tangled threads.

"Here are the five dead bodies, the three bridegrooms dressed in dark clothes, gray, blue and black. The lawyer, the military man, and the doctor and the two adventurers. They don't manage to separate themselves; they don't let you forget. Look at them, you can see them." Aunt Adelaida must be leaning forward as though she saw them clinging to a branch at the bottom of the well, because right away her stammering exclamations of surprise can be heard. "But it's not a question of bad luck. It's a very old wound made by a woman. Think even of those closest to you: relatives, friends. If you come three Fridays in a row we'll untangle it, as long as it wasn't done with a toad. If it's by toad it takes more time, because we don't know where it is buried, in order to unstitch it. But it's worth the trouble. See? If you do it, the sixth suitor will appear right away and this one won't die: this one is alive and well. The king confirms this. It's not a great love like the others, not even a great match, or a paragon of virtue. But, well, not everything comes up roses, gold and ivory."

"But in that case, why do I want him? What do I need him for?" Aunt Adelaida protests weakly.

"Oh! A man is good for a lot of things. Don't make me spell it out. And you wouldn't have to live in someone else's house, where you're always an intruder and you have to hang your head low and swallow jibes and insults and humiliations, and besides..."

"What tall tales are you making up? I live with my mother, my sister and my brother-in-law," Aunt Adelaida breaks in, her voice harsh, interrupting her companion's insidious drone.

"Your mother judges others as though she were living in the Old Testament, your sister is a snob, and your brother-in-law is a martyr."

Cora takes my hand and pulls me back firmly. Just a few steps and when we turn around we're back by the screen, close to the inferno and its luminous luminarias, and while María Teo's voice recedes, almost inaudible now, biting her words and spitting out bits of snake ("his head full of smoke," "haughty as a queen," "that man deserved a better fate," "but we all have to get on in the world"), I see the two shelves with rag dolls lined up, each one behind a lit candle in front of a glass of who knows what kind of water. There are lots of them; more than twenty, I think. At first sight they could all look alike. The homemade look follows elementary rules of a repeated basic anatomy: white faces with embroidered eyes and mouth, two dots for the nose, a rigid trunk of a body with hands and feet closed like fists. They all look female, with sketchy clothes and colored scarves or turbans on their heads, except for two or three that wear pants and something around their temples that looks more like a scarf than a cap. The general look is crude, but there are exquisite details, definitively added onto the basic model: an occasional birthmark, three colors of eyes, some marks that look like scars, even a few pairs of eyeglasses. As for needles, the quantity and the locations where they are stuck vary from one to the next. Some chests and heads are bristling with them.

There is something perverse, something unhealthy, in this incomprehensible spectacle. This enigmatic and inexpressive legion must serve diligently to achieve the most indiscriminate ends. And those sickly lights do not illuminate beatitude or channel prayer toward those with halos; they don't tremble agitated by the white feathery wings that ascend and ascend, but rather they wink desperately, asphyxiated by the dark membranes that suck them downward. I have to get out of there so the nets of that greasy anxious smoke don't entangle me and definitively carry me off to the underground caves of bats and damnation. And without lingering longer, I leave in a hurry, trying not to make noise. Whatever world I'm at the threshold of, it's a matter of saving skin or soul, but without attracting the guardians' attention.

"Who's there?" María Teo's voice sounds out in a long cry of pain, turning her attention from the vehement discussion that has absorbed her all this time, and of which I've heard only the dissonances, the sharp variations of the counterpoint.

No doubt she's turned her head and has immediately shoved the door back, without getting out of her chair, but Cora is already where I am, and it seems as though she ran and got ahead of me to block the path of any supposition, because above the distant murmur that has replaced the argument she says:

"What a dummy! How unbearable and totally stupid! What do you think they are? They're dolls in the place of people, so that the people can recover or get lucky and yet obtain what they want. She's explained it all to me perfectly clearly. You can't keep all those ladies and gentlemen at the house for all those hours and hours with a candle lit and praying, when they have to be in their houses, at the office or at the club. That's why the dolls are here. The dolls are working for them. Each one is a person. Do you understand? Images of saints stand in for the saints themselves, right? Well, it's the same thing. What were you scared of?"

"I don't know; I don't like it. It seemed to me as if the spiders were laughing. It seemed to me like a party in the devil's church. And what are all those needles for? And all those glasses?"

"The needles are to point to where the trouble is. So the almighty powers won't get it wrong. Don't they put pins in your clothes when they have to be adjusted? And don't you get injections when you're sick? And the glasses are just glasses, just that, so you know. Are you scared of glasses?"

Her logic is irrefutable, disarming, and there's no way to hide my stupidity.

"No, but I wouldn't want to play with those dolls. I wouldn't know who they are."

"I know perfectly well who they are, but when I play with them, they're dolls, nothing more. Or do you think that the widow Davis is the widow Davis and I bathe her even if she doesn't want that, or that Miss Eleanora has to sit and do penance because she doesn't even know where mother-of-pearl comes from, and that Mr. Almada eats my little meals and sleeps in the sewing basket? You don't really believe that?"

No doubt she decides there's no point in bothering to further enlighten someone as ignorant and hopelessly dumb as I am, because she shrugs her shoulders to end the discussion, looking more like a cabbage than ever, her attention fixed on the distance, and is as precise as a witness who is trying to reconstruct the complete truth:

"They were arguing. They've been arguing for a while. And even though they closed the door, they kept arguing. Now they've shoved back their chairs. They're opening the other door and here they come."

Yes, they're coming. There's Aunt Adelaida hurrying forward with that decisiveness that only deeply hurt feelings give her, and with that dignity that would cause the velvet to blush, in any fancier room than this worn-out sampler of clashing wools and complaining wicker. She thrusts her way forward like an irrevocable force, like a sailing ship, like a statue of majesty insulted by the idiocy that follows her in the form of María Teo, an ogress disguised in fallen eyelids and opprobrious smile, a bandy-legged freak who swings her hips defiantly to the very limit of balance, a malicious and provoking succubus with all the charm of an oozing sty, as my future indignation would make clear to me.

Aunt Adelaida's face is a model of expressions—anger, resentment, embarrassment, scorn—when she exclaims:

"Let's go! Not a single minute more in this viper's nest. Or who knows what we'll catch," while she grabs me by the arm and pulls me toward the entrance and keeps mumbling, "I don't know how I put up with this riffraff spying on my fate—and insulting me on top of that."

We could hear little sickly-sweet twittery laughs, a gabbly echo like a mocking parody and some words that sneak insidiously into the drawn-out tone:

"Go on, go on and make little dresses for the saints, you conceited fool. Buy patterns wholesale. It's better than killing off your fiancés, you poisonous creature."

And above everything, palms clapping, a foot tapping the rhythm, and the ever-higher voice following us like a fistful of needles:

"Chinese jellyfish, Chinese jellyfish, Chinese jellyfish."

The ones I have are different, but that doesn't mean anything. They probably have other clothes and other features because they come from strange cities and they represent characters in complicated stories in which there are always abandoned women and gentlemen who flee in swift carriages and white or black gauze that floats in forests and deserted houses full of wandering shadows animated by tides of vengeance or madness. They probably already completed their tasks or else their tasks have no point because they involve people who have already departed or who never will arrive, people in the windows of trains passing in the night without stopping even though a lantern is waved at them. Because those are the faces they have: faces made to simulate a presence for just a moment and then disappear. Except that here they lack accomplices to help them escape their roles. Here they don't have María Teo making them "work" as Cora said, making them be and stop being another person, and then when they no longer have any message to bear or to bring, they remain fixed in that absent expression that's so insistent it looks like pretend. If it were like that, if the moment really were to have gone by, they would be harmless, because they'd be uninhabited, like the others at those times when Cora plays. But I'll never be able to know that. And so in the meantime I'd better keep an eye on them, because sometimes it seems to me that I discover in them certain provocative intentions, that I don't yet know will inspire Balthus, like that way they have of sprawling around with their skirts tumbled, in those attitudes of abandon and shamelessness that must shock anyone, and that later will seem to me to have served as models for Balthus himself. I've also observed in Melania a certain propensity to exaggerate her lameness, especially during electric storms and every time one of those insects appears that makes you think of a stone set in a certain movement. Gervasia, for her part, never loses a chance to shake her head disapprovingly and even with repugnance when someone talks about certain illnesses or piles my plate with varieties of creamy and undefined vegetables while extolling their virtues. More than once I've come upon Adelia looking fed up at the other two, as though her high status doesn't allow her to live with them: two refugees, almost homeless people, taken in out of charity. She's more of a spy than anybody, with her ostentatious trousseau and her pretentious "Fait en France" that is so off-putting.

But with all this, aren't I trying to stall and put off saying as long as possible that this morning, with the complicity of someone I know, I wrapped up a package and sent it as a gift to Cora? María Teo will know what to do with them.

The Goodbyes

. . .

Now everything is tumbling us along, as if we were being hustled out of paradise: the bird that stays behind, the stiff and discolored grass, the lightning speed with which it travels the rails, vehement, unstoppable. With my forehead pressed against the window, I look into the reflection of the kissed face that will be remembered. I barely smile, and I cry silently.

Yesterday afternoon after Papa, Laura, María de las Nieves and her husband had already left for Bahía Blanca by car, I was still on the veranda of the nearly empty house, surrounded by packing crates and baskets. I was trying—but not very successfully—to laugh along with everyone else at Miguel's pirouettes, gestures and dances, seasoned with sad little spirit songs, voices like broken glass, and who knows what else, while his face—the face of the master of disguises—remained impassive, wearing the astonished and distant expression of a pale rubber mask. He'd often come up close to stare at me while he was working out his tricks and then I'd see a watery, intense, mirror-like shine in his eyes, and I could be almost certain that through the round opening of his mouth, his puckered or bitten lips were making an effort to hide their pain. Was I right? Might Miguel be one of those archangels designated by God to put obstacles on my path to the tree of life? And perhaps the protective oak, at whose foot I flung myself to escape from some grief, or hide from some punishment, might be my tree of life. No, that couldn't be it. Miguel's entire game was a farce to cover up his sorrow. The spectacle became unbearable to me. Curled up between two baskets filled with kitchen things, I spent the rest of the afternoon with a colander on my head, pulled over my nose like a hat, so I could see and cry better without anyone knowing. Mama, Grandma and Aunt Adelaida slogged away on the last of the packing, gave orders for sending the packages, oversaw the moving of furniture. At six they would come to get us to take us to Santa Rosa where we would spend the night.

At five-thirty the masked man discovered the girl who had hidden behind the dining room door and whom everyone had been searching for in the garden and all around the grounds. "What did you disguise yourself as?" he asked her in a low voice. "As Joan of Arc," she answered almost sobbing, remembering the illustrations of that story that was so sad. "And you?" "As a fireman, to save you." "I don't want to be saved. Besides, it's not true; that's not the right outfit." "No, and there's no fire, either. But look, in any uniform, I'm the guy who's going to look for you or wait for you until you come back," he said taking off his helmet and pulling off his mask. They were both in tears. He bent over, kissed her all over her face and licked up her tears. "Goodbye. Keep this until then," he said and he put a little stone into her hand. Her "Goodbye" was smothered under a moan, as was the whispered "Don't forget. I can't, I can't..." What was it she couldn't? The words were compressed, pushed out of order, asphyxiated by a contraction, but a knot was pressing against the inside of her throat. He hugged her tight, then pulled away fast and went running off.

Now I'm traveling with that little shiny, smooth black stone held tight in my hand. They'd have to open my hand by force to see what I've got there. It will travel miles and miles with me and I'll keep my fist clenched, almost crippled for seventy two hours. Then after that no one will have any idea what it's about. I'll say it's a talisman that a magician gave me. But it will continue to travel with me for many long years: miles and miles of written paper, of blank paper awaiting its poem, with that little stone tight in my hand. I don't know if it has a secret, a meaning that I don't know about. Sometimes it seems to me that it smells of something more than cold stone or that it beats like a tiny heart, as if inside it contained a miniscule bird; sometimes I feel a vibration as if it were trying to dictate to me the word I want to write, the word in whose search I keep writing. I still haven't discovered that is the word murmured by everything I look at.

Goodbye, house of fireflies, house of sheltering hidden corners, of mysterious and tangled forests. From your center, and you're the center of the world, if we'd had a ladder to climb up, we'd have been able to reach the center of the sky. But without going so far, during the nights, as the lights were going out, you began to sway and move like a ship carrying us to the farthest and most secret places, through all dangers and temperatures, and you'd leave us off again, unharmed and safe, every morning, in the usual place. I've found you later in all the houses I've lived in, and I don't know how we managed to fit into them. You'd come out to greet me, house, from places you couldn't possibly be: a window would open in a pillar, a door would appear in the middle of the stairway, the cellar would loom up through the skylight, the dovecote would stroll through the living room dragging a big chunk of garden. Other times I've also seen you in bad shape, with your steps dragging and your forehead somber, and even so, I know that you've recognized me.

Goodbye, goodbye eaves with gutters, tall creaking windmill, so tempting for balancing acts, immortal leaps and unstoppable mountain climbing; goodbye field of sunflowers and pond of frogs, green and polished as precious stones, and of the others, the stripy ones, the Mary-of-Egypt frogs; goodbye, bird cemetery with your three canary graves, a jar of faded butterflies we killed without meaning to, out of ignorance, next to the gold ring Laura buried when she was pretending to be a drowning, pursued buccaneer. Goodbye trees of our naptime escapades with your green fruit and your branches full of predatory human guests; goodbye, sandbanks by the Pirate Tower or by the remains of the castle from which the lookout, or my knight, will keep calling out my name that immensity will transmit from cloud to cloud, or from year to year, until the possible day; goodbye, glow of the smoky kitchen that makes giants of the fantastic shadows of Grandma's stories and harbors our blazing games and our agitated hearts on winter afternoons. I say goodbye to it all with the dazzled eyes of Iphigenia on her way to be sacrificed, and everything is already wrapped in the splendor of lost possessions.

Because in reality she's saying goodbye to everything she thinks will end. And could she ever possibly bear what is ending? She wouldn't even be able to bear the fatal spectacle of History. Cleopatra, Giordano Bruno, Anne Boleyn, will not die in the movies. They will keep fulfilling their destinies, after their "apparent" ends, as protagonists of other scenes in other films, in varied readings and even in the streets, in unsuspected corners. Sometimes the images will be indirectly connected: the intrepid tamer of snakes, the young hero who has sought refuge in a cabin by the fire, the woman who's had the neckline of her dress cut down. But if these links are missing, it doesn't matter. Any action and any person can serve to enable these lives to continue. Is that where my faith in the ultimate unity of everyone began, the belief that we are all one?

Now she believes that as soon as she turns her head, the breeze will have stopped blowing. Inexplicably, that won't be there anymore. She doesn't yet know that she will keep bathing with all her possessions in the same river or that she will continue submerging herself with all her stories in the different rivers she crosses. Every field, every cow, every flock of birds, every plant that spreads out its length across that unbridgeable distance that removes her, will continue to renew itself and fade away with her as she grows, as she ages. This separation is an ax blow of fate (alas, there will be so many) and she will never be able to recover innocence by means of forgetfulness, because an untamable, avid, fierce memory will be her weapon against the contingencies of time and of death.

But how far will she be able to stretch this ribbon or this elastic band that carries her along? And how many things will she be able to place in that immensity in order for everything to be close by and familiar, so no insurmountable holes, voids, or foreign presences will intrude? There will be room there for even what she thought unrecoverable or alien to this moment: the gilded chocolate pot with enamel roses that got smashed and is now restored, unchanged; the various little animals from her wooden zoo that strayed, gathered together again and lined up along the long road; the alphabet from beginning to end, end to beginning, several times; the little figurines of Chinese clay that make up entire populations in their boxes of millet seeds; the bright images stored away in envelopes, books and notebooks, the multiplication tables with their empty spaces and their errors, the collection of herbs she never managed to complete; the hallucinatory dolls, never trustworthy when peered at closely. Luckily, memory of the world is inexhaustible when it's a matter of filling and overcoming distance. Not to mention the most beloved faces or that stone she clenches in her fist and that multiplies itself endlessly in everything she looks at. And what will happen if the ribbon or the elastic band that carries her is cut or contracts? What might happen? We'll be returned to the starting point; we'll never stray again from where we are.

The child cannot know that between her and that place she left wrapped in grief and gnawed at by impotence, entire continents will seep through, with their flora and their fauna, other equally heartrending farewells, miraculous encounters, desperate insomnias, celebrations like fireworks, loves, moves, fires, births, futureless dawns, before she will meet up with Miguel again. It will be more than forty years of images passing across various sets of eyes looking at each other without finding those they were, until he might say solemnly, ceremoniously distant, as if all decked out in black, "Your house was a splendor and its people a source of pride for this town, and I, I had the extraordinary privilege of seeing them frequently." She yearned to ask, giving him the stone she still kept, "Was there someone who truly suffered when they left? Did someone go around like a wounded animal hiding in the corners?" but she restrained herself. "It would seem like a dream. Everything is so distant, so unreal, as if I were being told about it," he was saying, opaque, absent. "A dream? Didn't you salvage anything for when you'd awake? Not a feather, or a paper flower, not even mentioning something like the Grand Meaulnes jacket?" she thought. Nothing to salvage beneath the oblivion. There's nothing to say when rains of a hundred floods have fallen and the dunes have shifted a thousand times. Everything has been covered by sand, by another salt as hard as the kind that covered Carthage.

And here I am with the same helplessness, coerced into this journey. No one around to appeal to. They've allowed me to travel in my new dress, in order to cheer me. It's a blue dress, of fairly thick cloth, like a chilly sailor would wear, and I'm also wearing a hooded cape with important looking naval buttons. On the other hand, they haven't let me put my feet into Aunt Adelaida's high-heeled shoes that I tried to wear in order to somewhat cover my wounded child's dignity, but I've put on a great bandaid on my left wrist and another equally splendid one on a finger of my right hand. Of course they are showing off, the trappings of a nonexistent battle, but they console me a bit. Although no, I'm not consoled even by the enormous box of chocolate treats that Grandma gave me. But I'm comforted, at times, by her hand caressing my head slowly, very slowly, as if she were asleep.

Where did I almost fall? They've scooped me up out of the seat abruptly. We're leaving a remote, dusty station. Those kids that are playing jacks, squatting down on their heels on the platform, who are watching the train go by, who look at me and wave at me when I go past and wave at them, they're giving me proof that I'll come back again because in my mind, that's the bet I've made with myself when I lift and wave my arm: "If anyone waves back, I'll return." That white house, that cloud of smoke, that town blinking with its feeble lights, they're all my enemies. They will always be, in my memory, too, when I repeat this journey with three dead bodies who are now Mama, Grandma and Aunt Adelaida, with whom I'm traveling toward a place where four dead bodies are waiting for us in a house unfamiliar to me, four dead bodies then but who are now Papa, María de las Nieves, Laura and Daniel. It's startling to always be surrounded by dead bodies that are very pale, very still, who stare straight ahead as if on a train, on another train, although they're on the same one. It gives the impression that by knowing then when I'd return, when I'd come back, they already know now, and it's only me who doesn't know.

You don't know where you're going either, child; you'll never know. You only know that beyond all this painful suspense the sea awaits you. They've told you that the sea never ends, that its waves are the same as when the world began, that it ebbs and flows, ever ebbing and flowing. Deceptive, isn't it? Is everything unknown the same? Like a wild beast ever lurking, eager to attack and desist, waiting for the best moment to pull you under. Now it roars and calls you, and no doubt your tears become even saltier and it drags you, implacably, from some dark place in the future, like the solitude that came later and that will suck you in, that has already sucked you in, from some corner of the desolate future that blew out the lamps with a breath, darkened the crystals and covered you with inexplicable suffering from head to toe. "What's wrong? What's wrong with you?" they ask insistently, and sometimes they even enumerate some portion of all you have in order to show that you haven't lost anything. And you won't be able to explain that it's about something that isn't there yet, or that hasn't stopped being there, that it's something that will appear or vanish later, much farther along, something like the forewarning of sorrow for a happiness that will fade, a forewarning or a foreshadowed absence that already breathed in your face and was approaching you and absorbing you like the swirling winds of a blizzard.

It's true; I had no idea where I was going either. I will always believe I knew this after the fact, when I feel as though I'm starting out afresh. At every moment, I think that I now see ahead of us all the darkness that was behind us that I've already passed through, groping my way cautiously, with the instincts of a bat or with the long-range multiple vision of a cat. Sometimes I've gone a bit farther: I've compared the timeless darkness with the darkness of my soul, down to the last wall and the deepest depth, and they've been the same, and when fused, something like a spark has been produced, a revelation, an instant recognition, very fleeting to be sure, but something like the promise of a reunion or an enduring union with the ideal form, still invisible, in a place I came from and where one day I'll set foot and see and know. Meanwhile, even as I plumb the darkness amidst these glimpses of flares that approach me from the likeness to the image, I hold onto this faith and this hope. Here everything is done to bear the light through the shadow that spreads, and its full presence is only manifest in a flash of lightning, because it is not on this side. I am terrified by the single thought of trying to seize the enlightenment or full knowledge by hurling myself in one leap into an illusory bottomless clarity. It's like hoping to see the unknown face-on, from the center of a diamond, or like being a prisoner, encrusted in a blinding glacier, or worse yet, like leaping into an unbearable, hallucinatory brilliance, through which I fall and fall going nowhere, with no talisman, without a sacred thread, without a love stone clutched in my fist.

Against the false light that makes it impossible to see, I choose the invisible. Is that because the light, too, is an abyss?

Notes

Page 126: "St. John's Day Bonfires"

"Aserrín, aserrán" is a traditional song that originated in Spain but that is sung in different versions throughout the Spanish-speaking world, often as a lap-bouncing game like "Ride a Horse to Boston" in English. The song is also used in Spain and Latin America to accompany the ritual of dancing around a bonfire on the evening preceding Saint John's Day. The building of bonfires on June 24 is a practice of pre-Christian origin in Northern Europe, where the date coincides with the summer solstice. (It falls in midwinter in the Southern Hemisphere.) In the Christian era, this midsummer ritual was reconfigured as a celebration of the birthday of Saint John the Baptist. Although "Aserrín, aserrán" has many variants, Orozco uses the most popular version in the Southern Cone. The first word, aserrín, means sawdust, and the second word echoes it to form an onomatopoeic line imitating the sound of a saw. (Orozco's narrator herself suggests this with the interpolated commentary "'Hacen rin, hacen ran', imitando el sonido de la sierra"). The traditional version reads:

Aserrín, aserrán	Saw, saw
los maderos de San Juan	the woodcutters of San Juan
piden pan, no les dan,	ask for bread, they're given none,
piden queso, les dan un hueso	ask for cheese, they're given a bone
y les cortan el pescuezo.	and their necks are cut.

Lía quietly sings a more generous and less violent version to herself:

pide pan, se lo dan;	he asks for bread, he's given some;
pide queso, le dan un beso	he asks for cheese, he's given a kiss
y le acortan el almuerzo.	and his lunch is cut short.

In the last round, the children sing yet another variation:

Hacen rin, hacen ran,	They go "rin," they go "ran,"
los maderos de San Juan;	the woodcutters of San Juan;
pide pan, se lo dan;	he asks for bread, he's given some;
pide queso, le dan un beso,	he asks for cheese, he's given a kiss
y le apartan el escuerzo.	and they take the toad away from him.

Olga Orozco

Olga Orozco is considered to be one of the major South American writers of the twentieth century. Born in Toay, La Pampa, Argentina on March 17, 1920, she spent most of her adult life in Buenos Aires, working in journalism, radio, and education. She wrote poetry from childhood on, and was widely recognized as an outstanding poet. She is often considered as part of the "'40s Generation," sometimes called the Third Vanguard, a group of remarkable poets influenced by surrealism, Rimbaud, Nerval, Baudelaire, Milosz, Rilke, Neruda, and in Orozco's case, San Juan de la Cruz. She won over a dozen major prizes and awards, and her poetry appeared in hundreds of anthologies, and has been translated into at least fifteen languages. She also wrote short stories, many of which appeared in two major collections: *La oscuridad es otro sol* (1967) and *También la luz es un abismo* (1995). These stories portray, in highly subjective, impressionistic, and oneiric language, a childhood spent in a small town on the Argentine pampa. A few of these have appeared in anthologies or magazines, but they remained for the most part untranslated before the present volume. Olga Orozco died in Buenos Aires on August 15, 1999.

Olga Orozco's most important books:

Desde lejos. Buenos Aires: Editorial Losada, 1946.
Las muertes. Buenos Aires: Editorial Losada, 1951.
Los juegos peligrosos. Buenos Aires: Editorial Losada, 1963.
La oscuridad es otro sol. Buenos Aires: Editorial Losada, 1967.
Museo salvaje. Buenos Aires: Editorial Losada, 1974.
Veintinueve poemas. Anthology, prologue by Juan Liscano. Caracas: Monte Avila Editores, 1975.
Cantos a Berenice. Buenos Aires: Editorial Sudamericana, 1977.
Obra poética. Buenos Aires: Ediciones Corregidor, 1979.
Mutaciones de la realidad. Buenos Aires: Editorial Sudamericana, 1979.
Antología. Buenos Aires: Centro Editor de América Latina, 1982.
La noche a la deriva. México: Fondo de Cultura Económica, 1984.
Páginas de Olga Orozco seleccionadas por la autora, prologue by Cristina Piña. Buenos Aires: Editorial Celtia, 1984.
Antología poética. Madrid: Instituto de Cooperación Iberoamericana, 1985.
En el revés del cielo. Buenos Aires: Editorial Sudamericana, 1987.
Con esta boca, en este mundo. Buenos Aires: Editorial Sudamericana, 1994.
También la luz es un abismo. Buenos Aires: Emecé, 1995.
Antología poética. Buenos Aires: Fondo Nacional de las Artes, 1996.
Eclipses y fulgores: antología. Prologue by Pere Gimferrer. Barcelona: Lumen, 1998.
Relámpagos de lo invisible: antología. Prologue by Horacio Zabaljáuregui. Buenos Aires: Fondo de Cultura Económica, 1998.

A bilingual selection:

Engravings Torn from Insomnia: Selected Poems. Translated by Mary Crow. Rochester, NY: BOA Editions Ltd., 2002.

About the Translators

Mary G. Berg grew up in Colombia and Peru, lived in Spain, has taught Latin American literature (Ph.D. Harvard, Romance Languages), Latin American studies and translation at the University of Colorado at Boulder, UCLA, Caltech, and Harvard. She is now a Resident Scholar at the Brandeis University Women's Studies Research Center, where she worked closely on the preparation of this text with student Gilda Di Carli, whose readings, suggestions, and revisions were most useful. Berg teaches at Harvard Extension and has published extensively on Colombian, Peruvian, and Argentinean writers, with particular interest in women's fiction. She has participated in collaborative projects that reevaluate the writings of Latin American women, among them volumes published in Venezuela *(La ansiedad autorial)*, Colombia (*Narrativa colombiana del siglo veinte, Las Desobedientes, Escritura y diferencia, Escritoras de Hispanoamérica*), Chile, Cuba, Argentina, Spain and the U.S. (*Yo con mi viveza, Spanish American Women Writers, Portraits of Latin American Women Writers, Reinterpreting the Spanish American Essay, Women Novelists of the World*). Her recent translations include three anthologies of recent Cuban fiction (*Open Your Eyes and Soar, Cuba on the Edge, New Cuban Fiction*), poetry by Antonio Machado, Juan Ramón Jiménez and Carlota Caulfield, novels by Martha Rivera (*I've Forgotten Your Name*), Laura Riesco (*Ximena at the Crossroads*), Libertad Demitrópulos (*River of Sorrows*), and texts by Laidi Fernández de Juan, Clara Ronderos, and Marjorie Agosín.

Melanie Nicholson holds a Ph.D. in Hispanic literature from the University of Texas at Austin. She is currently Chair of Spanish Studies at Bard College, where she specializes in twentieth-century Latin American literature. She is the author of *Evil, Madness, and the Occult in Argentine Poetry* (2002), a study of the esoteric traditions in the poetry of Olga Orozco, Alejandra Pizarnik, and Jacobo Fijman. Her essays on Spanish American poetry have appeared in *Latin American Literary Review, Letras Femeninas, Crítica Hispánica, Revista Hispánica Moderna,* and *Studies in Twentieth and Twenty-First Century Literature,* among others. She has published translations in *Translation Review, Yale Review, Puerto de Sol, Denver Quarterly,* and *Contemporary Women Authors of Latin America: New Translations.* Her book, *Surrealism in Latin American Literature: Searching for Breton's Ghost,* is forthcoming from Palgrave Macmillan.